“What is it about you?”

Uneasiness crept over Ellie as she fished for her shoes under the car seat. “What do you mean?”

Mark looked over at her with an exasperated expression. “I mean you drive me to do crazy things like making out in the front seat of my car at a business dinner!” He turned back to stare ahead. “After all these years of keeping my nose clean, my boss suddenly thinks I’m Mr. Happy Pants.”

Ellie sat up angrily and snapped open her purse to retrieve her comb. The pheromone pills fell into her lap, and she froze. Beside her, Mark still muttered to himself. She coughed nervously. “Are we still going in?” She looked at him hesitantly. “I’m game if you are.”

“Yeah,” he said, straightening his tie. “It’ll look worse if we don’t.” He gave her a sheepish grin. “Thanks for being a sport.”

At the door, Mark rang the bell, then smiled at her as they waited. “I’ll have to admit, the garter belt was a nice surprise.” He rocked back on his heels, the picture of confidence again.

Ellie couldn’t resist knocking him off balance. “Then I can’t imagine what you would have thought of my tattoo.”

Dear Reader,

Happy Valentine's Day! I hope you are enjoying a happy and romantic month.

Harlequin is romance, so February 14 is an extraspecial day for us. Some people say it with flowers, others with chocolates, others with expensive jewelry, but those three little words, *I love you,* are perhaps the best words in our vocabulary. And at Harlequin, we get to be part of this experience all year long!

As a treat for this special day, what better way to recall the joy of falling in love, than with our Love & Laughter selection this month. RITA Award-winning author Marie Ferrarella spins a delightfully comic tale of identical cousins (they walk alike, they talk alike...) and the man who doesn't know which woman he's in love with! Talented newcomer Stephanie Bond hits a hilarious note in *Irresistible?* Single and dateless Ellie Sutherland, who considers Valentine's Day *Black Friday* (I know those of you who are single on Valentine's Day can relate!), takes *scientific* action to land a man.

Wishing you much love—and laughter,

Malle Vallik
Associate Senior Editor

IRRESISTIBLE?

Stephanie Bond

Harlequin Books

TORONTO • NEW YORK • LONDON
AMSTERDAM • PARIS • SYDNEY • HAMBURG
STOCKHOLM • ATHENS • TOKYO • MILAN
MADRID • WARSAW • BUDAPEST • AUCKLAND

ISBN 0-373-44014-6

IRRESISTIBLE?

This edition published by arrangement with Harlequin Books S.A.

Printed in U.S.A.

Stephanie Bond's friends, family and fellow computer programmers are usually surprised when they discover she writes comedy. After all, computer nerd and comedienne aren't typical hand in glove occupations. "Actually, I'm sometimes amused by the whole idea myself," she says, laughing. "I'm not an especially funny person—I'm just one of those people that funny things happen *to*."

When Stephanie isn't in front of her computer working or writing, (she admits there's so much food in her keyboard that it crunches when she types), she's usually boating with her husband, Chris, or at home near Atlanta, contemplating the grime on her windows.

Stephanie would love to hear from her readers. Write to her at 6225 Song Breeze Trace, Duluth, GA 30155

Many thanks to Natalie Patrick and Beth Harbison
for giving me a leg up;

To Rita Herron, Hillary Bergeron and Mary Barfield
for the weekly cheerleading;

And to Chris Hauck, for providing a constant
source of comedic inspiration—our marriage.

1

ELLIE SUTHERLAND opened her mouth to speak, but the sound that emerged was more like a croak. "I'm fired?"

Her supervisor, Joan Wright, coughed lightly, then leaned forward to rest her elbows on the desk. "Not fired. With the new budget cuts, I'm afraid we have no choice but to let you go. In one week," she added sorrowfully. "Please don't take it personally."

"I don't believe this," Ellie mumbled, shaking her head. *How am I going to make the rent?*

"Ellie, yours is not exactly a dream job."

"Oh, great," Ellie said. "I'm fired from a job that sucks, and that's supposed to make me feel better." *Credit cards. Food.*

"You know what I mean, Ellie. You're overqualified to be a gofer in a dumpy little federally funded arts center. You're too talented."

"Yeah, that's why gallery owners are beating down my apartment door." *Utilities. Painting supplies.*

"You'll get your break. Just hang in there. You know as well as I do it takes talent, luck and perseverance to make it in the art industry. And since you have incredible talent, you only need one of the other two qualities."

Tears pricked the back of Ellie's eyelids. "I had a feeling when I woke up this morning I should just stay in bed." She sighed. "I'd hoped to make some contacts at this job."

Joan brightened. "You did—me. I'll see what I can do about throwing some commissions your way."

Ellie raised her head to look over at the woman who'd become a friend in the short time they'd worked together. She could tell Joan felt bad about the turn of events. Ellie summoned her best what-the-hell smile, rose to her feet and said, "I'd appreciate it."

"Let me buy you lunch," Joan offered, glancing at her watch.

Ellie shook her head. "Thanks, but I'll be poring over the want ads." She trudged toward her tiny cubicle and grabbed her purse. She couldn't afford it, but she'd go out for lunch today and save the bagged egg-salad sandwich for dinner. Right now she needed the time to think.

She walked half a block to her favorite gourmet deli, then admired the handsome order taker as she waited her turn. The hunky guy in the apron was no small part of the reason this was her preferred lunch stop. When she stepped up to the counter, she took her time ordering a salad. The guy scribbled her order on a pad, then studied her intently. Ellie smiled demurely, enjoying the unexpected attention.

"You've been in here before," he stated simply.

"Several times," Ellie confirmed, sucking in her stomach and turning at a more flattering angle. She saw his nostrils flare as he leaned toward her slightly and inhaled.

"May I ask what kind of perfume you're wearing?"

Ellie fought to suppress the smirk that teased the corners of her mouth. Maybe this day wouldn't be a total loss, after all. "It's my own special blend. I worked on it for months to get it just right."

The attractive man smiled wryly and scratched his temple. "I just realized I get a migraine every time you come in here. I figure it must be the perfume."

She stood stock-still, her eyes darting sideways to see how many people were privy to the remark. Several customers snorted to cover their laughter and the buxom, vacant-eyed blonde behind her looked downright triumphant.

Ellie paid for the salad as quickly as possible and slunk to a table by the door. *Will this day ever end?*

She sighed as she sipped her diet cola and skimmed the wedding announcements. Starting with the life-style section had seemed like a good way to cushion her journey to the classifieds. But rather than enjoy the snippets about impending weddings, Ellie miserably counted off the handsome men with straight teeth who were now officially out of circulation in the city of Atlanta. She conceded the pictures also proved a little less female competition existed, but a new crop of coeds graduated every spring to catch the eyes of marriageable men. And spring commencements were upon the city.

She winced. Twenty-nine and dating wasn't so bad. But twenty-nine without a prospect in sight was downright depressing.

The bell on the door tinkled, announcing another customer. A stiff gust of unusually warm May air rushed over Ellie's table, lifted the page she'd been reading and wrapped it around her head. She clawed at the sheet with her hands, battling the breeze. After a few seconds of flailing, she tore her way clear, sneaking a glimpse at the person who'd just entered.

Her pulse jumped in appreciation of his profile. His dark head was down, alternately consulting his watch and a day calendar spread on his palm as he joined the long line snaking toward the counter. Ellie frowned at the expensive drape of the olive-colored Italian suit and turned back to her mangled paper.

Why do the cute ones always look as if they were just stamped out with a Donald Trump cookie cutter? Give me a great-looking guy who doesn't own a beeper and I'll give him lots of imperfect little kids. Where are all the good men, anyway?

A sudden jolt to Ellie's elbow sent her cola flying, dousing the paper, her salad and her lap. The icy liquid sluiced down her legs, stealing her breath. Ellie raised her arms, helplessly watching bubbly pools gather and run over the sides of the tiny café table to plip-plop onto the white tile floor. She squeezed her eyes shut and mourned the short life of the white linen skirt she'd scrimped for two months to buy. Then she stood and furiously spun to face the klutz who had ruined her lunch and her outfit.

Mr. Italian Suit had wedged himself between her table and another one, presumably to take a cellular phone call in peace, away from the din at the counter. He held one finger to his ear and stood with his back to Ellie. The big palooka hadn't even noticed his errant rump had wreaked so much havoc. Or worse, he didn't care.

"Hey!" Ellie yelled, reaching up to poke the man none too gently on his shoulder blade.

The man was just ending the call and turned toward her, his chocolate-colored eyebrows lifted in question. Ellie caught her breath. *Mamma mia.* He was gorgeous. Light brown hair with green eyes framed by those wonderful dark, dark eyebrows and lashes.

"Yes?" he asked, apparently still unaware of the soda puddling around Ellie's shoes.

Ellie opened her mouth to speak, and the phone started ringing again. The man muttered, "Excuse me," then flipped down the mouthpiece and said, "Hello? Yeah, Ray, what's up?" He glanced at Ellie and shrugged apologetically. Ellie stood, arms akimbo, and glared.

Of all the nerve! A few diners around her tittered and shook their heads. The hunky guy in the apron cast worried glances toward the spill. Well, Armani-man had picked the wrong day to mess with Ellie Sutherland.

She marched around to face him and jerked the phone from his unsuspecting hand. "Ray," Ellie spoke into the phone, "he'll have to call you back, sweetie." She snapped the mouthpiece closed, but held the phone out of reach when the red-faced man lunged for it.

"What are you, some kind of lunatic?" he thundered. "That was my boss—give me my phone!"

"No," Ellie said sweetly. "Not until you pay me for damages."

"Damages?" Confusion cluttered his handsome face. "What on earth are you talking about?"

Ellie swept her arm down dramatically to indicate her skirt.

The man stared blankly. "You're saying I did that?"

"That's right." Ellie smiled tightly. "And I have witnesses," she added, gesturing to the diners close by.

The man looked flustered, then sighed, withdrew a gold

usiness-card holder, flicked out a card and extended it to her. 'Send me the cleaning bill.''

Ellie pushed his hand away. ''No cleaning bill, mister. A ew skirt. You can't get cola out of white linen.''

The man looked briefly at her skirt and made a sound as if e didn't deem the garment worth saving. He ran his fingers rough his hair, obviously out of his element dealing with a int-size irate woman. ''How much?'' he asked finally, taking ut his money clip.

Ellie couldn't help doing a double take at the wad of bills acked there. ''Geez, mister, what are you doing carrying that uch cash around? You got a mugging fantasy?''

Every eye in the diner turned to the money in his hand. The ian looked around, then shook his head and leaned forward. 'Great,'' he whispered angrily in Ellie's face. ''That's just reat! Why don't you go out and tell everyone on the side-valk, too?''

Ellie balked and swallowed. ''Sorry.''

''How much?'' he asked through clenched teeth.

''Let's see…'' Ellie frowned. ''The skirt was brand-new. his is the first time I've worn it.''

''How much?'' he demanded, counting off bills. ''Fifty?''

''Well, then there's my salad and drink.''

''Sixty?''

''And my panty hose are sticky.''

The man inhaled a mighty breath and expelled it noisily. 'Here's seventy-five, and we're even, okay?''

''Okay.'' She took the money, grinning. ''Thanks.''

''Do you think I could possibly have my phone back now?''

''Oh, sure,'' she conceded with a generous smile, handing im the unit.

He snatched the phone out of her hand and gave her a final lare, then strode out of the deli without ordering. Immeditely, he began punching numbers as he walked by the win-ow and out of sight.

''Yuppie scum,'' Ellie murmured, counting the bills. ''What waste of good looks,'' she continued to herself, stuffing the ills into her wallet. She mopped up the table and herself as much as possible, ordered another soda, then begrudgingl turned to the want ads.

Jobs were plentiful on the north side of town, in Alpharett But Ellie didn't own a car and public transportation hadn't y caught up with the economic explosion in that area. She na rowed her job search to the few-mile radius surrounding h Little Five Points apartment. She could ride her bike if ne essary, or take the train. The pickings were slim, and the a tistic opportunities were nil. She had resigned herself to th waitressing section, when a blocked ad caught her eye.

> Wanted: Single women of any age with no current romantic attachments to take part in a four-week clinical study. Minimal time commitment. Above-average compensation. Must be willing to keep daily journal.

Ellie frowned. No current romantic attachment. She scanne the bottom of the ad to see if she was mentioned specificall by name. No, but it looked, sounded and smelled like her. Sh wondered briefly if it could be a scam to target unsuspectin women, but she recognized the address as a reputable clini Shrugging, she circled the ad with a red felt-tip pen. It wa worth a phone call. A glance at her watch told her she'd b better off to make the call from her desk.

The rest of the afternoon passed mercifully fast. Everyon had heard Ellie would be leaving, so in between expressin their heartfelt regret, co-workers piled last-minute remedi tasks on her desk. Somehow between photocopying, filing, an delivering mail, she managed to call the clinic to obtain a fe vague details about the study.

The woman who answered prescreened her with sever lengthy general questions. Ellie had to interrupt the intervie twice to answer other calls. After paging Joan over the inte com, Ellie feverishly punched a button to retrieve the woma she'd been talking to.

"Sorry—I'm back. Now, where were we?"

"Are you heterosexual, bisexual or homosexual?"

"Hetero."

"And are you currently romantically involved with anyone?"

"No."

"When was the last time you had sexual relations with a man?"

Ellie coughed. "Um, about a year."

"Can you be more specific?"

Ellie sighed. "Fourteen months, five days, and—" she checked her watch "—two hours."

"Very good."

Indignation flashed through her. "If you must know, no, it wasn't very good."

"That wasn't a question, ma'am," the bored screener replied.

Her cheeks burned. "Oh."

"There will be an information meeting tomorrow evening." The woman gave her the time and place, and the compensation rate.

Impressed, Ellie counted the days on her fingers until her rent was due, then asked, "When will the study begin?"

"As soon as enough participants register," the woman told her. "And you're the most ideally suited caller we've had today," she added cheerfully.

Ellie's eyes rolled. "I'm thrilled for us both," she said, then slammed down the phone just as Joan walked around the corner.

"We're thrilled for you too, Ellie," she said, fighting a grin.

"How much of that did you hear?" she asked, embarrassed.

Joan started to respond, but was interrupted by a yell from John, the accountant who sat two cubicles over from Ellie. "No more than anyone else, Miss Fourteen Months, Five Days and Two Hours." Choruses of hoots and cheers all over the department backed up his belly laugh.

Her eyes darted to Joan. "The intercom?" she whispered.

Joan bit her lower lip and nodded sympathetically.

DESPITE THE FRIGHTFUL DAY, Ellie's spirits rose on the walk home. Yes, it was incredibly expensive to live in downtown

Atlanta. Yes, traffic was a nightmare. And yes, in summer the humidity was unbearable. But it was worth every inconvenience to be part of the supercharged atmosphere. Ellie loved the outdoor cafés, the street musicians, the colorful murals, the unique shops. People-watching was one of her favorite pastimes, and the eclectic mix of residents that made up the artistic and somewhat affluent area of Little Five Points always provided a treat for the eyes. Atlanta was a wonderful place to live. Now if she could just find a decent job.

Ellie pulled her keys from her purse as she walked down the hall to her apartment. When a motion in front of the door caught her eye, she gasped. "Esmerelda, what are you doing outside?"

The tabby meowed an indignant reply, and Ellie scooped her up, hurriedly glancing down the hall. Her landlord would probably evict her if he discovered she was breaking the no-pet rule.

"It's me," Ellie yelled as she walked in. She could hear Manny in the kitchen. Dumping the cat on the couch, she said, "Esmerelda must have gotten out when I left this morning." She headed in the direction of enticing aromas, her pet pouncing off the sofa to follow her.

"Naughty puss," Manny chided, shaking a long finger at the cat. "Bad day?" he asked when Ellie flung her purse on the table.

Ellie suddenly felt close to tears. "Would being fired and having my new skirt ruined qualify?"

Her roommate clucked and came over to give her a hug. "You'll find another job," he said soothingly. "And that skirt—" he examined it with a thoughtful eye "—we'll dye it black and no one will ever know."

Ellie laughed. "You're an incurable optimist. Can't you let me be depressed for even a little while?"

He shook his blond head. "No. Now go change. I'm trying something new for dinner."

Ellie stopped long enough to unwrap her uneaten egg-salad sandwich for Esmerelda, then walked the few steps through the living room and down the hall to her bedroom. Manny

Oliver was a gem. They'd been friends for three years—in fact, his friendship with Joan Wright had landed Ellie the job at the arts center in the first place.

He made his living doing cabaret shows in drag. Ellie had seen him perform many times, and stood in awe of his singing, dancing and his killer legs. Her male roommate looked better in stockings and heels than she did. And if that wasn't bad enough, the man could cook, too.

After Ellie had changed, and joined Manny in the kitchen, she recounted her day over a scrumptious meal of Italian potato dumplings.

"Men are dogs," he supplied when she described the deli disaster.

"He gave me seventy-five bucks," she said, grinning.

"But rich dogs can be housebroken," he amended, and they both laughed. "Was he divine?"

She nodded, the image of the man's face forming in her mind. "Definite model material."

"Nice dresser?"

"Immaculate."

"Straight?"

Ellie shrugged. "I think so, but who knows these days?"

"*Tell* me you got his name," Manny pleaded.

"No, he offered me his card, but I smacked it away."

He shook his head. "Ellie, how many times do I have to remind you, the game is *hard* to get, not *impossible*."

She laughed. "He wasn't my type at all, Manny. A real stuffed shirt. I'll bet you couldn't get a toothpick up his—"

"Ellie!"

"Well, you know what I mean. Except for his obviously better taste in suits, he reminded me of the way my dad used to be—a corporate robot."

"People change, Ellie. Look at your dad. The man sees more naked people than a doctor."

"Yeah," she said with a short laugh. "Imagine my mom and dad retiring next to a nudist colony. It *was* by accident, you know."

"Oh, sure, Ellie, what would you expect them to tell their

daughter? If they didn't know about the nudist colony when they moved there, why haven't they posted a For Sale sign in the two years since?"

"I don't want to think about it. The whole situation brings to mind pictures I'd rather not see."

"The point is, your dad finally mellowed out."

Ellie snorted. "After thirty years of missing family dinners and undergoing two bypass surgeries." She stabbed another dumpling. "My mom should have left him decades ago."

"He's a good man, Ellie, you said so yourself."

"He neglected his family."

"But your mom was always there for you."

Angry tears welled in her eyes. "But who was there for her?"

Manny reached over and laid a hand on her shoulder, giving her a light shake. "They're happy now, Ellie. Save it for your therapist." He took a sip of wine, then asked, "So what are you going to do about rent money?"

Leave it to Manny not to mince words. "I called about an ad for participants in a clinical study. The money sounds good—I'm going to find out more about it tomorrow night." She told him about her conversation with the screener. Manny laughed and agreed it sounded promising.

"You've got a guardian angel on your shoulder, Ellie. How else can you explain losing a job, then finding a want ad for desperate women on the same day? A toast!" He lifted his wineglass to hers.

Ellie stuck out her tongue at him, then good-naturedly clinked her glass to his.

THE MEETING ROOM WAS more crowded than Ellie had expected. Based on the cramped accommodations, the crowd had apparently surpassed the clinic's expectations, as well. The room resembled a college classroom: no windows except the tiny one in the door, fairly new, dense low-grade carpet in a speckled gray, and filled with more folding chairs than the fire marshal would probably care to know about. A large blackboard covered the entire front wall. The side walls were adorned with various-size corkboards bearing dozens of multicolored sheets on topics ranging from sleep disorders to impotence.

Ellie lowered her dark glasses and, as inconspicuously as possible, peered at the other women in the room. She judged her appearance to be somewhat better than the room's average, and the observation depressed her even more. She pulled down her floppy hat and slumped in the hard metal chair.

Opening her pocket sketchbook, Ellie flipped through to find a clean page, always ready to draw the face of the person nearest her for a few minutes' practice. Her hands stilled at the page where she had sketched a caricature last night. Mr. Italian Suit with the gooey dark eyebrows smirked back at her, a cellular phone clutched in his cartoon hand. His athletic body strained at the savvy suit, miniature in comparison to his big, good-looking head. Ellie studied the rendition of his eyebrows and nose and wondered how close she'd come to capturing his true expression. If she remembered when she got home, she'd add a smudge of green to highlight those brooding eyes.

At that moment, a bespectacled, lab-coated woman walked to the front of the room and raised her arms to hush the chatter.

"My name is Dr. Cheryl Larkin. I'm a medical doctor, and a professor of human behavior, and it is my privilege to oversee this clinical study. Each of you has been prescreened to a certain extent to qualify for a four-week experiment using pheromones, chemicals produced in animals which attract other animals of the same species."

Ellie sat up. Her own experiments in perfume making had overlapped into the area of aromatherapy. She had become intrigued with the idea that certain scents could be aphrodisiacs. Supposedly, pheromones went even further.

The doctor continued. "Pheromones are subtle but powerful secretions. Some people say they explain the elusive chemistry that attracts a specific man to a specific woman, and vice versa. The objective of this study is to see what effect, if any, oral pheromones have on your ability to attract and meet a romantic interest."

Ellie glanced around and saw that Dr. Larkin had the undivided attention of every woman in the room. Hope shimmered in the eyes of the shy, the overweight, the very short and the very tall. She swallowed because she knew her own baby blues reflected the same emotion.

"It will be necessary for participants to answer a lengthy and somewhat personal questionnaire, and to keep a daily journal detailing encounters, or absence of encounters, for each day." A spirited buzz broke out in the room as applicants whispered excitedly to strangers next to them. Ellie ignored the gleeful exclamation of the middle-aged woman beside her.

"The dosage is two pills first thing in the morning, around midday, and again at bedtime. Besides the aforementioned hypothesis," the doctor said, finally smiling, "there are no proven side effects with this particular formula. We will ask, however, that participants be especially aware of and record any changes in your energy level or in your eating and sleeping patterns."

An arm shot up near the front. "Let's say I take these pills and meet a great guy. You're telling me after four weeks the rug gets jerked out from under me?" Everyone laughed and the doctor joined in, then raised her hands defensively.

"Wait a minute—we can't guarantee you'll meet even one eligible man during the course of this study. If that were true, we wouldn't need the experiment at all."

Intrigued, Ellie nodded. This could be fun. After the doctor had finished her talk, Ellie stayed to fill out the necessary paperwork and wait for a counselor to administer the dreaded questionnaire. Three hours later, she emerged with a week's worth of pills and a small blank journal in her purse, feeling as if she'd just been to confession. But she noticed a new spring in her step. She believed in the powers of aroma. Pulling off the hat and dark glasses, she tossed her short blond locks.

Unsuspecting men of Atlanta, beware!

"WELL, Marcus, if you're not going to get married, you're going to have to learn to cook," Gloria admonished her son as she held a dripping whisk.

Mark Blackwell plucked a green olive from the tray on the kitchen counter and popped it into his mouth, smiling. "I like to eat out."

The plump woman turned back to her bubbling red sauce. "It's beyond me how, out of all those women you've dated, not one of them could find her way around a kitchen."

"I don't—" he walked over and took the whisk from her hand "—date women for their culinary skills." He flashed a grin in his mother's direction.

"Oh, you," she snorted, rapping him playfully on the arm. Then her tone grew more threatening. "If you're not careful, you're going to grow old all by yourself."

"I'll hire a comely young nurse," he teased. "Besides, you'd be bored if you couldn't fret over my state of bachelorhood all day."

"Not if I had grandchildren," she replied with a twinkle in her eye.

Mark didn't miss a beat in the familiar exchange. "You're much too young to be a grandmother."

"And you're much too young to be working yourself to death in that law firm," she chided.

Mark grabbed two plates and settled them onto his arm, waiter-style. "That's what I came to talk to you about," he said, smiling. He dished up a hearty helping of lasagne for each of them, and spooned on the rich homemade sauce. When he set the laden plates on the table, he struck a cocky pose and said, "Say hello to the newest partner of Ivan, Grant, Beecham, and...Blackwell." He bowed slightly, rewarded with enthusiastic applause from his seated mother.

"How wonderful, Marcus!" She beamed and brought his hand to her mouth for a long kiss. "I'm so proud of you, son. I wish your father were here." Tears sprang to her eyes immediately, but she blinked them away.

Mark swallowed the lump of emotion that lodged in his throat. He knew his father would be proud of him at this moment, even if Mark *had* "caved to the corporate philosophy," as his flighty father was fond of saying. Ever the softheart, his dad had been struck by a car three years ago when he'd stopped to help a stranded motorist. Mark patted his mother's hand. "I wish he were here, too," he said simply, then smiled. "Now, let's eat."

During dinner, they chatted about his long-awaited promotion, but Mark had a feeling he wouldn't escape without at least one more lecture on the importance of finding a good woman. Especially now that he'd made partner. He was right. As he helped his mother clean the dishes, she said in an innocent voice, "You know, the family reunion is this weekend. Are you coming?"

"Yes," he said patiently. "Don't I always?"

"Hmm," she agreed, then asked, "Are you bringing a date? Your cousin Albert will be there with his new bride and baby. And Claire with her newborn—this is her third, you know. Her husband is such a dear man."

"I can't wait," Mark said, inwardly wincing. He considered these get-togethers his penance for bucking the long family tradition of having a houseful of kids before having a house. He would endure one whole day of shaking hands and exchanging cheek kisses with new family members. And dutifully praising and holding everyone else's kids while his mother drank wine in a corner and her sisters tsk-tsked over her woeful lack of grandchildren.

"So, are you bringing a date?" she asked hopefully.

"I'm definitely bringing a change of clothes in case Mickey's little one has the runs again."

Gloria covered her mouth and shook with laughter. "The video he took of you two is just precious."

Mark rolled his eyes heavenward. "I'm awaiting my debut on one of those home-video shows."

"Stop changing the subject. Are you bringing a date or not?"

His thoughts shifted to Shelia, the woman who'd last graced his bed. She hadn't struck him as a woman who'd appreciate the rural pleasures of pitching horseshoes and doing the hokey-pokey. Neither did Vicki, Connie or Valerie, come to think of it. "I'll see what I can do," he said. It was as close to a promise as he could make. Suddenly, a vision of short blond hair and flashing blue eyes came to mind, and he frowned. "I'm not really seeing anyone right now."

Gloria clasped her hands together gleefully. "Stella's niece is in town for the Sunday-school teachers' convention—shall I give her a call?"

"No," Mark said quickly, then recovered. "I have a lot to do at work this week, you know, rearranging my office and all that. I'll be working late every night."

His mother shrugged, clearly disappointed. "Suit yourself."

Later, Mark squashed down guilty feelings which threatened to surface as he drove home. He knew his mother wanted to see him properly settled with a nice, quiet girl, but he truly liked being single. He'd sacrificed his social life during law school and the first few years after joining his firm in order to get a foothold. Now at thirty-six and established in his career, he was enjoying his unattached status. Life was good.

He almost managed to drive by the interstate exit to his office, but he merged onto the ramp at the last second. Just a few minutes to go over some paperwork, he told himself.

After he unlocked the office suite, he walked across the glossy inlaid wood floor not without a measure of pride. He considered the law office tastefully furnished, with just the right amount of opulence. His new office space had been achieved by removing a supply room adjacent to his existing office. He had been asked to select additional furniture, and he was pleased with his pecan wood and cream marble choices.

The Piedmont Park painting had been hung, and he approved of the location. One of his favorite pieces of art in the law office, he'd requested it for his own work area when the move began. He flipped on a floor lamp near his desk, and settled into his familiar tan leather chair to shuffle through the stack of papers on his desk.

Congratulatory memos comprised the top layer of paper. A box of cigars and an expensive leather-covered pen set were gifts from thoughtful colleagues. He smiled in satisfaction. Everything he'd worked for had finally been realized. He would never have to struggle like his father just to make ends meet.

Clasping his hands behind his head, he leaned back in the swivel chair to prop his feet on the corner of his desk, basking for a moment in the recognition of his hard-won achievement.

Partner.

At a sound from the doorway, Mark turned his head. Patrick Beecham stood there, holding the hand of Patrick, Junior. "Hi, Mark," Patrick said, his voice full of surprise. "Pretty late to be working."

Mark rearranged himself into a position more appropriate for talking. "I could say the same," he said to his partner with a smile.

"I just stopped by to get a fax," Patrick said. The small boy pulled on his father's pant leg. "This is Pat, Junior," he added.

"I remember," Mark said. "He's growing like a weed. How're you doing, buddy?" he asked the boy.

"Okay," the child ventured, half hiding behind his father.

"Say, Mark," Patrick said, "Lucy and I would love to have you over for dinner sometime. Do you have a lady friend?"

"You sound like my mother," Mark said. "Are you two in on a conspiracy to get me settled down?"

Patrick laughed. "No, but I must admit it helps to have someone presentable when socializing with the other partners and clients. I'll warn you—Ivan kind of expects it."

Mark felt a sudden swell of anger that anything would be expected of him other than top-notch work. "I like being unattached," he said evenly.

"So did I," Patrick admitted. "But there comes a time when we all have to grow up. Luckily for me, Lucy was there when I came to my senses." He swung the little boy into his arms. "Just food for thought, friend," he said absently, tickling the little boy until he squealed. "Don't work all night, and let me know about dinner, okay?"

"Sure," Mark said. "Sounds great."

Mark listened to the footsteps fading down the hall, and pounded his fist lightly on his desk in frustration. What idiot had said behind every successful man was a good woman? He'd made it this far on his own, and he wasn't about to share ıe fruits of his labor with some money-hungry man-eater. Ie'd seen the way women's eyes lit up when they discovered e practiced law. He'd seen them peruse every stick of fur-iture in his home as if assessing its worth. He bought nice ıings because it made him happy, not to impress women. And e resented the females who thought he'd be all too eager to ırn over his possessions to their care. Demanding, all of them. 'ake that little chiseler in the deli the other day—seventy-five ucks for a scrap of fabric!

Where could he find a woman who'd settle for a no-strings-ttached arrangement to be his escort, in return for a few nights n the town and an occasional romp? Oh, sure, they all said ıey weren't looking for a commitment, but after a few dates, ʋhammo! Feminine toiletries and articles of clothing started ɔ appear in his house, and every jewelry commercial seemed ɔo clever for her to let pass without a remark. Where was it ʋritten every man was supposed to settle down with one ʋoman and be content for the remainder of his days?

He resumed his propped position and nodded his head in ilent determination. *Bully for the poor schmucks who fall for ', but count me out.*

2

"WHAT DO YOU THINK?" Ellie asked, peering at the two shell-pink tablets in her palm.

Manny leaned forward, sniffed at the pills, then said, "I think if these little pills can make you irresistible to men, then I want in on the action."

Ellie scoffed. Manny was tall and slim, with a handsome face. On more than one occasion, female acquaintances of Ellie's had offered to try to "convert" him. "Manny, you've got more dates now than you know what to do with."

"But none of them are keepers," he said, sighing dramatically.

"What do you consider a keeper?"

"Anything below eight inches gets thrown back," he declared, making an over-the-shoulder motion.

Ellie shook her head, grinning, and pulled a clean glass from the dishwasher.

Manny's forehead knitted. "This is what—the fourth day you've been taking those things?"

"Uh-huh," she said, tossing the pills into her mouth and downing them with a swallow of fruit juice.

"Shouldn't something be happening by now?" he asked, watching her face carefully. Suddenly his eyes widened, and he covered his mouth to muffle a scream.

"What?" Ellie yelled, shoving past him to run to the hall mirror.

"Gotcha," he called, doubled over laughing.

"Oh, very funny," she said after a reassuring glance in the mirror. "You're a regular comedian, Manny."

"Gotta run," he said, heading for the door. "Good luck on your last day at the Smithsonian," he joked.

Ellie pantomimed a drumroll. "Ba-dump-bum."

Friday at last. When she walked to her overflowing closet, she toyed with the thought of wearing something ratty—what did it matter? Then she spotted her pink-and-black-checked mini. Why not go out with a bang instead?

With renewed vigor, she pulled on black hose, clunky-heeled pumps and a long, white knit cardigan. She buttoned up the lightweight sweater so she could omit a blouse, then added large earrings, funky bangles and a handful of gold chains around her neck. She slicked back her pale hair with gel, then traded her regular beat-up canvas bag for a soft shoulder-strap briefcase and a small silver purse. At the last second, she remembered to skip perfume, lest it interfere with the pheromones. When she stopped in front of the mirror on the way out, she nodded. Not bad for a gal down on her luck.

She held her head higher than usual when she stepped onto the sidewalk. Not quite seven o'clock on a beautiful May morning, and suited pedestrians already clogged the walkways. A few well-trained individuals even read the morning paper while their feet moved and stopped automatically at crosswalks. Ellie shook her head in determination. She would never get caught up in a seven-to-seven job like a lot of people she knew, like her father.

It had taken two bypasses to convince him to change his workaholic ways. He'd wasted so much of his life cranking out numbers for a big-eight accounting firm. If not for her mother's patience and virtue, their marriage would never have survived. And less than a year of the bureaucracy at the hole-in-the-wall arts center where Ellie worked convinced her she wanted no part of a rigid office setting on a long-term basis. Still, the regular, if small, paycheck had paid her rent.

An oncoming dark-suited banker type lowered his stock quotes long enough to admire Ellie's legs and whistle. Her spirits rose and she shrugged guiltily. Okay, it didn't hurt her feelings to be *appreciated* by the well-heeled.

With the money from the study to tie her over for a few

weeks, she planned to spend her free time updating her portfolio, and pestering gallery managers to take a peek. Being fired might turn out to be the best career move she'd ever made.

The aroma of bagels and cream cheese reached her, prompting her to dig in her bag for loose change. "Ellie!" old Mr. Pompano exclaimed. "You look good enough to have for breakfast, yourself. Did you get a promotion?"

"No," she said smugly to the popular street vendor, pointing to a chocolate bagel. "I got fired."

"Well, it suits you." He smiled, handing her the dark bread. "You are especially—" he made a corkscrew gesture in the air "—appealing today."

"Why, thank you, kind sir who wants my money." She curtsied.

He grinned and bowed slightly, then patted his right knee. "Something good will happen to you today—I can feel it in my gimp leg."

Ellie winked. "Can your bursitis tell me if he'll be a blond, a brunette or a redhead?"

"The way you look today, *Cara,* you might get all three."

Ellie flipped him a quarter tip, and munched her bagel the rest of the walk to the musty office building where she worked. Several men's heads turned, eyes lingering, and she felt her body unconsciously adjust to the attention. Her short stride lengthened to show off her legs. She thrust her shoulders back and her small breasts out, and clenched her buttocks with each step to add a powerful sway to her back view. It worked. She'd heard two wolf whistles by the time she reached her office, where a handsome co-worker, Steve Willis, who'd never even glanced her way before, held the door open.

"Ellie, isn't it?" he asked, his pale eyebrows arching attractively over his tortoiseshell-rimmed glasses.

"Yes, but I'm afraid I don't know your name," she lied.

"Steve," he said, straightening the knot of his tie. "Steve Willis. I was thinking, maybe I could call you sometime?"

"Sure," she said nonchalantly over her shoulder.

"What's your number?" he called behind her.

Ellie turned to eye the man who'd gone out of his way to ignore her when she'd delivered his mail every day for the past year. She almost felt sorry for him—he didn't stand a chance against the pheromones. "I'm in the book," she said simply, and left him standing. Once she got around the corner, she brought her fist to her chest in a triumphant gesture. "Yes!" There was something to these pills, after all.

The flowers on her desk were a nice surprise. She knew they were from Joan even before she opened the card. But before she had a chance to thank her boss, the phones started ringing, and the day began.

Later, a few co-workers took her to lunch, and Steve Willis appeared out of nowhere to sit beside her. He even managed to knee her a couple of times under the table. Feeling generous, Ellie humored him with a smile. He really wasn't bad. Maybe Mr. Pompano's gimpy prediction had been right.

Joan stopped by Ellie's desk an hour before closing. Ellie smiled, gesturing to the flowers. "I meant to swing by to say thank you."

"You're welcome. I wanted to talk to you before you left."

Ellie turned her swivel chair toward Joan. "What's up?"

"A commission, if you're interested." Joan leaned against the cubicle wall.

Ellie nodded enthusiastically. "Sure."

"It's a corporate portrait for a law firm—pretty boring stuff, but good money."

"Suit-and-tie picture?"

"Yeah."

"How did you hear about it?"

"I know the wife of one of the partners. I've acquired a few paintings and a couple of sculptures for their office. It's the same company that bought your Piedmont Park scene, by the way."

Landscapes were Ellie's forte. Although she enjoyed painting portraits, as well, she preferred a little creativity with the subject's presentation. Still, it was a job. She smiled and nodded to Joan. "Sounds great."

Joan handed her a card. "Here's the name of the firm and the address. I've written the agreed fee on the back."

Ellie turned over the card and her eyes bulged. "I get to keep this?"

"Less the ten percent cut for the center, yeah," Joan said. "Consider it a severance bonus."

"Gee, thanks."

Joan glanced at her watch. "If you leave now, you can get over there before they close."

The women said their goodbyes and Ellie promised to let Joan know how the commissioned painting progressed. Stopping by the apartment, she dropped off a box of accumulated desk junk and her briefcase. After taking a few minutes to freshen up, she walked to the street to hail a taxi.

"Where to?" the heavyset man yelled, looking her up and down with appreciation.

Ellie told him the address and climbed into the back seat. During the ride, the talkative driver hinted at his single status. Ellie, enjoying the attention but not wanting to encourage the man, simply smiled and said, "That's nice."

He screeched to a halt in front of the building, and she got out. He leaned out the window and said, "Miss, do you mind telling me what kind of perfume you're wearing?"

Ellie rolled her eyes. "Let me guess—it gives you a migraine?"

The man looked confused. "No, I'm serious."

Ellie opened her mouth to tell him about her own special blend, then stopped short. "I'm not wearing any," she said, suddenly remembering.

"Yeah, sure, lady," he said. "Whatever it is, I hope my date is wearing it tonight when I pick her up." The man tipped his hat, waved away her fare and drove off.

Ellie stood on the sidewalk, perplexed. She raised her wrist to her nose and sniffed. Nothing, just skin. She shrugged, glanced up at the towering building, then walked in.

When she exited the elevator onto the appropriate floor, Marcus Blackwell's name was being gilded onto the double glass doors. The graphic artist seemed to be having a heck of a time repositioning the firm's name on the door to work in all the letters. If they added another partner in the future, they'd have to install a third door, she thought wryly.

Ellie sighed, wondering how much money would be squandered by the firm to herald the addition of Mr. Blackwell. A new sign, new company stationery, an expensive portrait. Must be nice.

His secretary was beautiful. More like gorgeous, really. The woman's nameplate said Monica Reems.

"May I help you?" she asked.

Ellie frowned. Nice, too—how despicable. "I'm Ellie Sutherland. I'm here to see Marcus Blackwell about painting his business portrait."

"Is he expecting you?"

"No, I'm sorry, he isn't. I received the assignment only a half hour ago and I was hoping to catch him before he left for the day."

The woman smiled, displaying—what else?—model teeth. "He's in a meeting, but he should be out any minute. Have a seat and I'll make sure he knows you're here as soon as he gets back."

Ellie sat down and studied her surroundings. Ivan, Grant and Beecham were doing very well for themselves. And of course, Mr. Blackwell, the latest rising star of the firm. She tried to picture him—early fifties, salt-and-pepper hair. Eyeglasses, probably, which were always a pain to paint because of the glare and because they made the eyes seem flat. Dark suit, no doubt. Small gray teeth. Or bright white dentures. And one or two prestigious rings—Harvard perhaps, or Michigan. Very ho-hum, but relatively easy.

Begrudgingly, she conceded the office decor was impeccable. A little stodgy, but first-class leather furniture and textured wallpaper. And honest-to-goodness artwork. Ellie wondered where they'd hung her Piedmont Park painting, and prayed it wasn't in the men's room. She'd heard those things happened. From her position, she could see the door to the men's room at the end of the hall. As minutes clicked by and boredom threatened to settle in, she became convinced her painting adorned the wall. Over the urinals.

She sneaked a peek at Monica, who had her back turned and the phone crooked between her shoulder and ear. It would take only a few seconds to check, and she hadn't seen anyone go in the entire time she'd been seated. After one last glance at the busy secretary, Ellie sidled down the hall, then pushed open the heavy door, straining to hear voices or other sounds of activity. Silence. She stepped inside.

The outer room was a lounge of sorts with inappropriately elegant furniture. Ellie began a hurried search of the walls. There were several framed prints, most of them architectural, but she didn't see her painting. She sighed in satisfaction. An arched doorway led into a tiled room of more predictable sterile-looking gray Formica stalls. Three individual urinals lined an adjacent wall, and Ellie eyed them curiously. "I've always wondered," she muttered. Her voice echoed, and she jumped. Then another sound reached her, approaching footsteps from the outside hall. Sweat immediately broke out on her upper lip.

Searching frantically for cover, Ellie dived into a stall and slammed the door behind her. Then she realized her pump-clad feet would be a dead giveaway because the door didn't extend all the way to the floor. She jumped up and straddled the black seat of the commode, crouching so her head couldn't be seen.

The man who entered whistled tunelessly, probably celebrating the forthcoming weekend. When he stopped in front of her stall, Ellie held her breath. She could see the shadows of his feet and legs. At last, he walked away from her hiding place and stopped near the urinals, she deduced. Sure enough, she heard the slide of a zipper and the sound of urine splashing against porcelain. Ellie grimaced and prayed he had a small bladder.

What if someone else came in? What if a whole crowd came in at once? She'd be trapped listening to a herd of men relieving themselves!

The man peed. And peed. Ellie rolled her eyes. This guy

belonged in the record books. And just when she thought he'd stopped, he started again with the same gusto. Her arms began to ache from balancing herself between the slick walls. She repositioned herself slightly forward to relieve her shoulder pain, and caught a glimpse of the marathoner's back through a tiny slit in the closed door. Her hand slipped and she caught herself, thumping lightly against the stall. She jerked back and held her breath, then relaxed. He seemed to be conjuring up a grand finale, too occupied to hear her.

Finally, the man zipped his pants and flushed the urinal. Ellie listened as he washed his hands slowly and seemed to dry them just as slowly. He walked by her stall on the way out, and she grew weak with relief.

Then she dropped her purse.

Most of the contents were emptied on the first bounce, then the silver bag rolled out of sight. Makeup, coupons, pens and miscellaneous items scattered everywhere. She watched a tampon slide until it stopped by a leg of the stall. She closed her eyes and waited.

At first there was no sound at all. Then the man took three slow steps back to stand in front of her door. And he knocked.

Ellie swallowed. "Y-yes?" she managed to get out.

"The ladies' room is down the hall." His voice vibrated deep, distorted with echoes.

"I, uh, I didn't know this was the men's room," she improvised.

"Are you standing on the toilet?" he asked, incredulous.

She carefully stepped down and straightened her shoulders, then addressed the man through the closed door. "No," she said, and bent to retrieve the strewn articles within her reach.

He'd bent to pick up the purse and the items laying outside the stall. He wore nice shoes, soft black leather loafers with perfect tight little tassels. On feet big enough to make Manny salivate.

After a few seconds, he asked, "Are you coming out?"

"I'd rather not," she confessed.

"Okay," he said, his voice booming. He sounded close to laughter. "I'll put your purse on the counter and leave."

Ellie waited several seconds after the outer door closed before she moved. She opened the door and scooped up her purse, quickly checking the floor for wayward keys or coins. Then, praying fervently the man wasn't waiting outside, she swung the door open and stuck her head out.

No one in sight. Uttering her thanks, she trotted down the hall and reclaimed her seat near the still-distracted Monica. When the secretary ended her phone call, Ellie stood and asked, "Has Mr. Blackwell returned?"

Monica shook her head. "Any minute now, I'm positive." The phone rang again and she answered it quickly.

Ellie sighed. Then, hearing someone approach, she turned, and inhaled sharply. Mr. Italian Suit. The yuppie who'd ruined her skirt! What was *he* doing here?

Still several feet away, the man slowed, his head tilted in question. Suddenly, his eyes widened in recognition, and he strode toward her, his forehead knitted. "Look," he said, making chopping gestures in the air, "I don't know how you found me, but I'm not giving you another red cent for that overpriced skirt you said I damaged."

Fury gripped her. Ellie drew herself up to her full height of five foot two inches and leaned toward the fool, ready to...to...muss his hair. "For your information, you big klutz, I have no idea who you are and I haven't been looking for you." She lowered her voice to a hiss. "I'm here to see a client and I hope you scram before he gets here because I'd like to make a good impression."

Blue eyes blazed into green ones as the silence mounted. Behind them, Monica hung up the phone and coughed politely. "Excuse me, Mr. Blackwell."

Ellie heard the name and the pieces fell into place. She felt the blood drain from her face. "You?" she whispered.

"Me, what?" he asked impatiently.

"You're Marcus Blackwell?"

"Mark Blackwell," he corrected. Turning to Monica, he asked, "What's going on here?"

"This is Ellie Sutherland, sir. She's here about your portrait."

He frowned and threw up his hands in a gesture of frustration. "I'm lost."

"Didn't Mr. Ivan tell you? Your portrait will go up in the boardroom beside the other partners'."

Mark Blackwell glanced from Ellie to his secretary. Ellie relaxed her stance and offered him an exaggerated shrug, smiling wryly.

"I'm not prepared for this," he said finally, in a guarded tone.

Ellie gave him a shaky smile. "This isn't litigation—there's nothing to prepare for."

He looked at her, chewing his lip. Obviously Mark Blackwell stood in unfamiliar territory, and didn't like it one bit. His eyes narrowed. "And how, may I ask, did you get involved?"

Ellie smiled brightly. "I'm an artist."

Mark rolled his eyes and sighed mightily. "Why doesn't that surprise me?"

She glared. "What's that supposed to mean?"

He waved dismissively. "Forget it, um—what did you say your name was?"

"Ellie," she said with growing impatience. "Ellie Sutherland."

He ran his fingers through his hair, a gesture she recognized from the deli incident. "Well, Ms. Sutherland, perhaps we can discuss this, er, project in my office." He swept his arm toward a door a few steps away and motioned for Ellie to precede him.

She stood her ground. "After you."

He pursed his lips, then turned and walked toward the door.

Ellie noticed the painting as soon as she entered the huge masculine room. She walked over to it, soaking up the familiar shapes and colors. An afternoon in the park. A cliché, really, but her first truly good piece. There had been others since, additional impressionistic renditions of city landmarks, but she had been especially proud of Piedmont Park and the price it had brought. She lifted a finger, and almost touched the canvas. "Nice picture," she murmured.

"Nice purse," he said sarcastically.

Ellie's hand flew to her bag as her eyes swung across the room to his feet. They were big feet, wearing nice black leather loafers with tight little tassels.

"Do you make a practice of skulking in men's washrooms, Ms. Sutherland?"

She felt a blush start at her knees and work its way up. She raised her scorching chin indignantly. "Certainly not. I told you, I didn't know it was the men's room."

"Sure." He smiled a disbelieving smile, then leaned on the front of his desk. "Now then, what do you need from me?"

Ellie turned and took a step toward him. Their eyes locked. And just like that, something passed between them. At least she felt it.

A shiver ran up her back, and a low hum sounded in her ears. Looking at him, she realized she'd done a shamefully good job of capturing his features for the caricature. His eyes reminded her of a length of dark green velvet she'd once bought just because she liked it. She'd hesitated to cut it, to tamper with the natural drape of the lush fabric. She'd ended up folding it across the footboard of her bed, unhemmed. Now every night when she went to bed, she'd be thinking about Mark Blackwell's eyes.

"Hmm?" she asked, completely oblivious to the reason she'd come here.

Mark shook his head, as if to clear it. "Um, I asked, what do you need from me?"

This time, his words were slow and coated with fresh meaning. Need from him? A hundred images galloped through Ellie's mind, and Mark Blackwell loomed naked in all of them. She could see the surprise in his eyes, the slight confusion lurking there. Then she remembered. Of course, the pheromones.

For an instant, disappointment fluttered in her chest. Then she recovered and walked closer to his desk, conjuring up a natural smile. "Just a few hours of your time, really." She paused for a moment, then said, "Do you have a favorite suit?"

"I never thought about it," he answered slowly.

"One you reach for when you have a very important meeting?" she coaxed.

He pondered for a few seconds, seeming embarrassed. "My olive one, I suppose."

"I've seen it," Ellie said, nodding her approval. "It's a good choice."

"Is this a new look?" he asked, eyeing her avant-garde hair and outfit.

Ellie recognized a diversionary tactic when she saw it. She looked down at her trendy, chic clothes. "Don't get out much, do you?"

His left eyebrow rose a fraction of an inch.

She blinked purposely and continued. "Wear the olive suit to the first sitting. Bring both a solid white shirt and an off-white shirt. And a handful of ties."

"First sitting? I'm afraid this is all new to me."

"I'll need you to sit for me for a total of about fifteen hours."

His eyes widened. "Fifteen hours?"

Ellie laughed and raised her hands in defense. "Not all at once. One or two hours at a time—whatever you feel up to. I'll take photographs to work from at home."

He scowled and folded his arms. "I'm not comfortable with this."

The toothpick remark she'd made to Manny came to her lips, but she bit it back. Instead, she said, "Just relax—I'm not painting you in your mallard-print boxers."

Mark studied her for a minute, the tiniest hint of a smile lifting the corners of his mouth. "I don't wear mallard-print boxers, but then I thought you'd know from your earlier vantage point in the men's room."

Ellie swallowed. Maybe he wasn't as uptight as she'd thought. "Briefs, then."

He shook his head. "Wrong again."

"Bikinis?" she squeaked.

Mark extended a finger and beckoned her to come closer.

Ellie did, and leaned forward for him to whisper in her ear. "Bare-assed."

Ellie jerked up and took a step back before she realized he was laughing at her.

"That wasn't very nice," she retorted.

"You fished for it," he said matter-of-factly.

"Where were we?" she asked, trying to reassume a professional stance.

"I was sitting for you."

"Shall we do it here in your office?"

His eyes raked over her body. "It would be a first, but sure."

Her pulse leaped. The image of them vibrating his desk across the room came to mind, but she stifled it. The chemicals she emitted triggered his reaction and she'd do well to remember that. She forced a serious face, refusing to verbally acknowledge his innuendo. "Fine. When?"

He still smiled, his eyes dancing. "Tomorrow morning at nine?"

"I'll be here with my camera," she said, already walking toward the door.

"You bring your equipment," he called to her. "And I'll bring mine."

Mark caught the flash of her silver purse being slung over her shoulder as she closed the door. Where had that idiotic comment come from? He jumped up and clutched his head with both hands, pacing. He'd never made suggestive comments to women he'd worked with. Willing women were plentiful, he'd never had to worry about mixing business with pleasure and risking a ruinous outcome. He cursed, rubbed his eyes, and walked the length of his office to his liquor cabinet. Appraising the newly stocked shelves, he selected a fine Kentucky bourbon, and poured himself a shot.

Tomorrow he'd conduct himself like the professional he was. He'd refuse to rise to her bait, no matter how enticing. The last thing he needed was for a nut like Ellie Sutherland to complicate his life.

3

"YOU'RE JOKING," Manny said, his eyes wide.

"Nope," Ellie declared, swallowing a bite of cheese omelette. "It was him, in the flesh."

"Was he as dreamy as you remembered?"

She nodded enthusiastically. "Absolutely."

"And single?"

Ellie frowned. "I didn't notice a wedding ring, and he was kind of...flirtatious. But that doesn't mean anything these days."

"You said it, girlfriend."

"He's too stuffy, and way out of my league. He probably has a black book full of women named Muffy and Phoebe."

Manny touched her forearm. "You're probably right." Then he grinned. "So why don't you introduce him to *me?*"

"Sorry," Ellie said, and pulled a sympathetic face, "but I don't think Mark Blackwell is your type, either."

"I can put on a skirt if he insists," Manny said, pouting.

"I'll see if I can work it into the conversation today," she offered sarcastically.

Manny lifted a sausage link to his mouth and bit off an end suggestively.

"You're a kook," she said, laughing.

"Me?" he asked. "Who's the one who sneaked into the men's room and listened to him pee?"

"I didn't see anything."

"Oh, so you did look?"

"No!" She grinned sheepishly. "Okay, I peeked, but I only saw a sliver of his back. Cut the wisecracks for a minute. I have to tell you the strange things that happened yesterday."

"I'm all ears."

Ellie told him about the incidents with men on the street, with Steve Willis, her co-worker, the taxi driver and some of the things Mark Blackwell had said to her. "And when I got home, Steve Willis had left a message on my machine. I haven't had *that* many men flirt with me in my lifetime," she asserted, reaching for the bottle of pink tablets. "It has to be these pheromones working."

"Well, aren't you glad they're working? What's the name of the manufacturer? I'm buying stock." He reached down to stroke Esmerelda's ears.

"Do you think I'm imagining things?"

"I think you're horny. You haven't had a relationship since...Drew, wasn't it? That was ages ago. I've forgotten, why did you end it?"

"His penis had attention deficit disorder."

"Oh, yeah, right." Manny nodded. "Well, if you want to see if the pheromones are causing all the hullabaloo, don't doll up today and see if you get the same results."

Ellie snapped her fingers. "Good idea."

THE LAW OFFICES of Ivan, Grant, Beecham and Blackwell were several blocks away, but easily accessible by bicycle. Ellie pulled on a neon green helmet that matched her bike, strapped on her backpack of supplies and jumped on to begin pedaling away her breakfast calories. No man could possibly flirt with her at this speed.

It was another beautiful day, too nice to be cooped up inside. She figured she'd be through with Mark Blackwell by noon, then she could spend the day sketching crowds at Underground Atlanta in preparation for her next portfolio painting. She stopped at a traffic light and waited for a police officer to wave her through the dense jam.

The police officer was within touching distance. And, she noticed, cute beneath his half helmet. He waved the traffic by on the side street, but his eyes stayed on Ellie the entire time, a whistle clasped between white teeth. She smiled at him and he smiled back. He waved through more traffic and studied her legs. She smiled. He waved through more traffic and winked at her. She winked back. Suddenly horns began to sound behind her from commuters impatient with the lengthy amount of attention the officer paid to the cars on the side street. Finally, he pulled his eyes away from Ellie and blew his whistle to halt the line of cars whizzing by. When she pedaled by, he lifted his hand to his helmet in a friendly gesture. Definitely the pheromones, she thought.

When she reached Mark's building, she took the elevator to his floor. The law offices were much quieter than the previous day, but still busier than Ellie imagined they would be for a weekend. On the other hand, Mark Blackwell probably worked Saturday, Sunday and holidays. To her surprise, more than one et of male eyebrows raised appreciatively when she made eye contact in the halls. Of course, she did look a little out of place wearing her cycling togs.

Monica's station sat neat and unoccupied, so Ellie stepped o Mark's office door and knocked.

"Come in," he called.

He sat at his desk, pen in hand. He glanced at his watch and said, "I was getting ready to check the men's room."

"Sorry," she said. "I had a flat this morning." She patted her bike, walked it over to the side wall and lowered the kickstand.

She pulled off her gloves and realized he was staring quizically at the bike. "No place to chain it up out front," she aid cheerfully. "I can't afford to have it stolen."

He pointed to the bags of dried herbs she'd picked up from street vendor on the way. "I hope you don't plan to smoke hat stuff."

Ellie glanced at the ingredients she'd purchased for a new perfume recipe. "Not here," she said, grinning wryly.

"Is that your night gear?" he asked, smirking, and indicated er neon clothing.

Ellie looked down at her pink bike shorts and bright yellow ank top. She had certainly dressed down today, complete with unning shoes. She pulled off her helmet and ran a hand through her short waves. "You can't be too safe in this traffic."

He stood, tossing the pen on a stack of documents, and tugged gently at his waistband. Ellie caught her breath. Mark Blackwell looked deadly in pleated olive slacks and an off-white shirt, open at the collar and revealing a shadow of dark hair. *Easy, girl. This is just a job.* His jacket hung from a light-colored wooden valet in the corner behind his desk. Several ties hung there, as well as a white shirt, still under the dry cleaner's plastic.

"I see you brought the things I suggested," she said, nodding her approval.

His eyes locked with hers. "I'm nothing if not obedient," he said in a tone which indicated that wasn't the case at all.

The undigested omelette flipped over in her stomach. "Well," Ellie said nervously, "let's get started, shall we?" She unstrapped her backpack and pulled out a folder. "I've taken the liberty of drawing up an employment contract."

Mark poked his tongue in his cheek as if he was amused but said nothing.

"Pretty simple stuffy, really," she continued. "It mentions the materials used, the fee and the delivery time frame of the portrait."

Mark reached for the document and read it quickly. His eyes swung up to her. "I would never have imagined painting to be so lucrative."

Ellie set her jaw and took two deep breaths. "It isn't. Jobs like this are few and far between. And I'm buying all the supplies, which includes framing the finished portrait."

"Still, it's a lot of money. You must be very good." He sounded doubtful.

Ellie bit her tongue, tempted to mention the Piedmont Park scene hanging ten feet from her, but the thought suddenly struck her that maybe he didn't even like the picture and had merely inherited it with the office. Instead of leaving herself open, she raised her chin, gave him a small smile and said, "I am *very* good."

Mark Blackwell chewed on his tongue for a moment. Then

cleared his throat. "What is a 'kill fee'?" he said, looking back to the document.

Ellie shrugged. "My protection. I do freelance photography for magazines, and I've been burned on last-minute publishing cancellations. This protects me if you—" She stopped and bit her bottom lip.

"If I'm run down by a beer truck?" he finished.

"You could say that, although I doubt if the term has ever been applied quite so literally."

"What if I don't like the painting?" he asked, laying aside the contract and folding his arms.

Ellie opened her pack and pulled out miscellaneous supplies, including a camera. "Satisfaction guaranteed," she said, smiling wryly.

He opened his mouth to speak, but a knock on the door stopped him. "Yes?" he called.

The door opened and a handsome, wiry, black-haired man stepped in. "Blackwell, about the Morrison deal—" He stopped when he spied Ellie, a blatant admiring look crossing his face. Glancing back to Mark, he said, "Maybe we can discuss this some other time."

Mark's face hardened. "After our conversation yesterday, Specklemeyer, I thought there was nothing left to discuss."

The tension between the two men hung in the air, almost palpable. "Perhaps I should wait outside," Ellie offered, starting for the door.

Mark stopped her, holding up his hand. "No." He glared at the younger man. "This won't take long."

Specklemeyer's shoulders went back and anger diffused his smooth skin. "Morrison is my client, and I intend to do what the man asked me to do."

Mark's voice hummed low and deadly. "You work for this firm, and you will do what you're instructed to do. If not, there won't be anyone here to cover you when the IRS comes calling for you."

The man's face contorted in a sneer. "Being partner has gone to your head already, hasn't it, Blackwell? Last week you were just a flunky like the rest of us, and now you think you have veto power.''

''You're wrong,'' Mark said calmly, refolding his arms. ''I *know* I have veto power.''

The other man's eyes narrowed, his fists balling at his sides. Convinced they were going to fight, Ellie moved her supplies back a few feet to the perimeter of the office, but when she glanced up, the younger man was stalking toward the door. He closed it with a resounding slam.

''Sorry for the interruption,'' Mark said into the ensuing silence. ''Tell me how this works,'' he said, waving an arm to encompass Ellie and her things.

''First I need to see the other portraits yours will be displayed with so I can maintain the corporate mood, so to speak. Your secretary mentioned it will be hung in the boardroom—is it close by?''

''Right this way.'' He led her out of his office and down a wide hallway. The boardroom sat dim and deserted this weekend morning. It reeked of old books. The overhead lights did little to brighten the dark paneled room, so Ellie opened all the blinds. Then she walked around the room, perusing the five large somber portraits adorning the walls. Two partners had apparently retired—or worse.

''Pretty standard stuff,'' she acknowledged, pulling a tape measure from her pocket and recording the size of the canvasses and frames. She glanced at the towering man beside her. ''Wouldn't you at least like to smile in your portrait? Remember, it'll be your legacy.''

Mark frowned. ''My legacy will not be a vanity painting on a wall.''

His vehemence surprised Ellie. ''You have children?'' It hurt more than a little to know he was married, after all.

The frown deepened. ''No, I don't have any children—yet.''

''But you're married?''

''No,'' he said, a bit flustered, then added, ''not yet.''

''Engaged?''

''Not yet.''

"Oh, you're one of *those,*" she said knowingly, then turned her eyes back to the painting in front of her, immensely relieved.

"One of those what?" he said defensively.

"You're a Peter Pan man. No wonder green suits you," she said, indicating his slacks.

His mouth opened, then closed. Pointing with his index finger, he said, "I don't believe this—*you* are psychoanalyzing *me?* And what is all this Peter Pan nonsense? Let me guess—*Cosmo's* feature this month, right?"

"There have been volumes written on men like you," she said, sashaying past him into the hall.

He caught up with her in a few seconds. She thought he'd be angry, but surprisingly, he seemed to concede defeat. "Do you by chance know my mother?" he asked. "Gloria Blackwell sent you here to torment me, didn't she?"

Ellie laughed as she reentered his office. "No, I don't know her, but I know someone just like her in Florida—Gladys Sutherland." She shrugged. "It's universal. It's what mothers *do.*"

One corner of his mouth went up. "Is your mother a matchmaker?"

Ellie snorted. "She's Chuck Woolery in a girdle."

He laughed. "Mine, too. The last woman she set me up with brought a book along to read."

Ellie threw her head back and laughed. "The last guy my mom set me up with informed me over a fast-food dinner that women were getting way out of hand and needed to be put in their place."

"Oooh," he said. "A real charmer." Their laughter peaked, then petered out as they looked at each other and realized they'd just shared a friendly moment.

"Well." Ellie cleared her throat, and moved toward her supplies. "I guess I'd better get to work."

"Just tell me where you want me," he said, hands on hips.

Ellie looked up and saw the implication in his eyes. He was tempting, all right. She measured her response. "How about in that straight-back chair by the table?'' *Which has always been a personal fantasy of mine.*

''Suits me,'' he drawled.

To her horror, a stab of desire knifed through her as she watched him swing his coat on, grab a tie and walk to the chair. She stood mesmerized as he efficiently tied a tiny knot at his throat. Watching his nimble fingers move was suddenly the most sensual thing she'd ever seen. Ellie moistened her lips with the tip of her shaking tongue. Few men could be this sexy *putting on* clothes.

The celibacy was making her behave this way. She'd gone too long without a man's body next to hers. And now, the first time a man with the physique of an exotic dancer came along, she fell to pieces. She wiped beads of perspiration from her forehead. ''Turn the chair sideways, and have a seat.'' She picked up the camera and busied herself attaching the lens, willing her pulse to slow.

At this rate, she'd be jumping his bones by lunch.

Mark eased into the chair and exhaled deeply. She was doing it again, throwing him sexual crumbs—and he was gobbling them up like a starved man. He clenched a fist to steady his nerves, but his traitorous eyes sought her out. How was it possible this woman could turn screwing on a camera lens into foreplay?

He had steeled himself against her this morning, but he hadn't counted on her wearing skintight elastic neon clothes. And little white crew socks with pom-poms on the heels. And for her hair to be so…mussed. He groaned.

''Are you okay?'' Ellie asked, walking toward him, concern on her pert little face.

''Uh, sure,'' he said, sitting straighter.

''First I'm going to rape you,'' he heard her say matter-of-factly.

Lights burst behind his eyes. ''Excuse me?'' he croaked.

''Drape you,'' she repeated. ''I'm going to drape you.'' She held several different-colored cloths over her arm and, picking up a navy one, shook it in front of him for emphasis. ''See?

I need to decide what color background would be the most flattering.''

Disappointment shot through him and he fingered his collar a fraction looser. ''Whatever you say,'' he said, laughing nervously. *Get a grip, man.*

Using small, capable-looking hands, she placed the navy fabric over his right shoulder. Her fingernails lightly nipped the back of his neck, and a gray swatch suddenly appeared over his left shoulder. Ellie stepped back to observe him, stepped forward to adjust the drapes, and back again, studying. She reached for her camera and snapped five or six pictures at lightning speed.

With eyes narrowed, she walked toward him and leaned forward. Suddenly her face was mere inches from his. He could see a freckle centered perfectly on the end of her nose, and for one crazy second, he thought she might kiss him. He parted his lips and waited. She grabbed his chin and adjusted his head, sharply, to the right. ''Don't move,'' she ordered, then started snapping more pictures.

''I can't,'' he said testily. ''I have whiplash.''

If she heard him, she didn't acknowledge it. If fact, her next adjustment to his head was even more severe than the first. ''Ow!'' he yelped. But she was busy focusing and clicking. More drapes appeared, this time red and burgundy, then dark green and gold. To pass the time, he'd been halfheartedly keeping track of the number of rolls of film she'd used. But as she draped him in a deep plum color, he'd gotten a chinful of soft breast, and the blood rushed from his brain to more urgent parts of his body. She reloaded. Did that make twelve rolls? Or twenty-one?

Ellie Sutherland turned into a different person when she worked. She was a study in concentration, utterly efficient.

''Smile,'' she ordered.

And she was devastatingly beautiful. He could imagine sliding those bike pants off and pulling her onto his lap, her straddling him wearing those delightful pom-pom socks.

''There's a good smile,'' she said. Click, click. ''Whatever it is you're thinking, keep thinking it.'' Click, click, click.

He could reach under that ridiculous yellow tank top and push it up to expose her to him. She'd have great tan lines, her breasts outlined perfectly, surrounded by sun-kissed skin. And her nipples—

"Hey," she said, lowering the camera. "The lurid grin suits you, but I don't think it's what you want for posterity, is it?"

Mark recovered with a start, and reined in his wayward thoughts. "Are you almost finished?" he asked somewhat brusquely.

"Just a few more," she said, bending down on one knee for a different angle. When she stood up a few seconds later, Mark breathed a sigh of relief. Finished at last, he hoped. Then she would leave. Out of sight, out of mind.

Ellie, however, reloaded again. "Now, let's try the white shirt and a different tie," she said without looking up.

Mark gritted his teeth. How much longer was he going to have to put up with her incessant teasing? He stood and walked past her to the valet, loosening his tie along the way. With his back to her, he unbuttoned his cuffs, then the front, and slid the shirt off his shoulders. As he lifted the plastic from the white shirt, he distinctly heard the camera go off. He swung his head, but Ellie was wrestling with the camera, pointing it at the floor. Her head was down.

Mark turned back to his new shirt, and heard two more clicks. Again he swung around and her face looked downward, contorted from her strenuous efforts with the suddenly temperamental camera. This time, when he resumed his task of removing the shirt from the hanger, he kept her in his vision in a mirror to his right. While he appeared to be absorbed in undoing buttons, she glanced at him over her shoulder, then turned, focused on his naked back and snapped two quick pictures.

Why the little voyeur! Then a thought occurred to him, and he grinned to himself. "Don't turn around," he said over his shoulder, rehanging the new shirt. "I must have sat down in talcum powder before I left this morning. Give me a minute to remove my pants and dust them off." In the mirror, he saw the back of her head jerk up. He unzipped his pants and made other noises of undressing, but left his slacks buttoned. Her head moved slightly side to side as if she was contemplating her next move. Just as she raised the camera and turned, so did he.

He heard two clicks before Ellie realized she'd been had. She straightened, her face flushing to a most becoming shade of deep rose.

"Are these for your personal collection?" he asked, crossing his arms over his bare chest.

Busted taking pictures of the man changing clothes! Ellie's mind raced faster than the heat growing in her cheeks.

Mark Blackwell stood completely still, except for a muscle that twitched beneath his left pec. God, the man was gorgeous. His shoulders were broad, his arms athletically defined, but not overly so. A tangle of dark hair covered his chest, his dark nipples slanted on firmly uplifted muscle. His waist was sectioned in flat planes of taut skin, which narrowed into his waistband. Ellie felt a single drop of sweat trickle between her breasts as she moistened her dry lips.

With an effort, she shrugged into a relaxed posture, then threw one arm up in what she hoped resembled a casual gesture. "It's not what you're thinking. Some people are more relaxed when they don't know their picture's being taken," she said in her most authoritative voice, bobbing her head for emphasis.

Seconds passed. Then a full minute. She willed her head to stop bobbing, but it jerked up and down of its own volition.

"If you'd gotten the picture you wanted," he said quietly, "you'd know just how *un*relaxed I am at the moment."

"I don't know what you mean. Can we get on with this, please? I do have other plans for today."

He eyed her for a few seconds longer, then a strange look came over his face. Reaching to tug on the white shirt, he said, "Sure." His face once again melded into a serious, professional mask.

Ellie frowned while he concentrated on his buttons. No wonder this guy was still single. Who wants a moody man? Up then down, hot then cold in a matter of a few seconds.

Then it hit her and she almost slapped her forehead in revelation. She kept forgetting about the pheromones. The poor guy didn't know what was going on. It all made sense now—his early teasing, and now suddenly pulling back, as if he'd just regained his senses.

She busied her hands with the camera, but kept one eye on him. His hands were slow on his buttons, and he seemed almost thoughtful. So intent was she on analyzing his silence, his voice startled her.

"Do you mind telling me what kind of perfume you're wearing?"

Bingo! "I'm not wearing perfume," she said.

Mark looked up and frowned slightly. "Scented lotion? Shampoo?"

Ellie shook her head.

"Are you sure, because I could swear..." His voice trailed off, and he shook his head in uncertainty.

"What does it smell like?" she asked. She could record his observations in her journal. The counselor stressed the importance of noting details.

"I don't know," he said. "It's hard to explain. Like...fresh air." He glanced at her, seeming embarrassed.

Ellie grinned nervously. "In downtown Atlanta? Your schnoz must be playing tricks on you."

"Right," he said, sliding on a tie and stepping to the mirror to complete the knot.

His phone trilled, causing Ellie to jump. Mark strode to his desk, glanced at the tiny number-display screen, then groaned.

"What?" Ellie asked.

"It's my mother," he explained, picking up the receiver. "Hi, Mom...yes, I saw your number come up on the screen." He looked at Ellie and smiled. "Yes, it's an expensive feature, but all the office phones have it...no, I don't know how much it costs, but it's worth it...yes, if I think of it, I'll ask Monica...yes, I promise."

Ellie giggled and motioned she was leaving to give him privacy. Mark shook his head and waved her toward a chair, holding up a finger to indicate he'd wind up the call in a minute or so.

"No, the name of the person calling doesn't appear, just the number...uh-huh...no, it wouldn't be possible for you to know if Stella was calling from Gert's house, Gert's number would still appear." He rubbed his eyes with index finger and thumb, clearly trying to remain patient.

Ellie enjoyed eavesdropping on his conversation. Even a senior partner could be reduced to childlike politeness around his mother.

"Mom, did you call just to talk about my telephone?" He frowned. "Oh. Sure you can ride with me and my date." He turned slightly away from Ellie and she couldn't see his face.

Ellie felt a tiny pang of jealousy. Which was ridiculous, she thought. It was only reasonable to assume a man like Mark Blackwell dated, whenever his hectic schedule allowed, that is.

"No, you don't know her...uh, a couple of weeks now... yes, she's nice...no, no children...no, I don't think she's ever been married, but the subject hasn't really come up...yes, I agree that's very important, but it just hasn't come up...you'll meet her tomorrow, okay? Look, I've got someone in my office, so I'll call you later, okay? I love you, too, Mom. Bye."

He hung up the phone with a heavy sigh, then turned a wry grin toward Ellie. "That was the infamous Gloria Blackwell."

"She sounds persistent."

"The IRS should hire her," Mark agreed. Suddenly his face brightened. "Hey, are you busy tomorrow?"

Ellie's heart skipped a beat. A date? In an instant she remembered the woman in the clinic who had asked about the chances of meeting a great guy and then having the rug pulled out from under her when the pills wore off. It would be too easy to lose her heart to Mark Blackwell. Plus, she wasn't about to get involved with a man whose arteries were probably already clogged with stress. And he'd only made the offer because he was under the influence of the pheromones. Self-preservation kicked in. "I'm busy every Sunday," she said.

"Working or playing?" he asked in a teasing voice.

"A little of both," she admitted. "I usually go to Underground and set up an easel to draw caricatures." Gathering courage, she stood and attempted to clarify the situation. "Look," she said earnestly, "you're not exactly my type and I'm probably not yours, either, so—"

"Whoa," he said, raising his hands. "It's just a family picnic. I'm in a bind and I really need a date."

"And I really need the money I'll earn at the mall," she said sincerely. *And you scare me to death.*

He leaned against his desk and drummed his index finger against his chin. "How about a business proposition?"

"What do you have in mind?" Ellie ventured cautiously.

"How much money will you make drawing at Underground?"

Ellie averaged her earnings from the last few times she'd worked there and added twenty percent. "About two hundred fifty dollars."

Mark whistled. "Two fifty? Okay, I'll give you three hundred to go to the picnic with me."

"Why?" Ellie asked, suddenly suspicious. "You could probably get a date just by picking up the phone."

"How good an actress are you?" he asked, smiling.

"I made a pretty convincing artichoke in my fifth-grade play. Why?"

"Because," Mark said, now grinning broadly, "I want you to be the epitome of my mother's worst nightmare."

Hurt speared through Ellie. "Excuse me?"

He stood up and walked toward her. "Don't take this wrong. But if we could convince my mom you're my new girlfriend and that we're completely wrong for each other, she might ease up a little and realize my being a bachelor isn't so bad, after all. Come on, it'll be fun."

Ellie balked. "I'm not sure if I'm flattered or insulted."

Mark took a step toward her with his arms extended. "You said yourself I'm not your type. Think about it. We seem to get along okay—"

Ellie snorted.

"Sort of, plus, I need a date with no strings attached, and you need the money," he finished triumphantly.

Ellie frowned. "I'm not for sale."

"Three hundred fifty."

"Shall I bring baked beans or potato salad?"

"UNBELIEVABLE! This man is actually paying you to go out with him?" Manny exclaimed, counting the bills Ellie handed him. "Do you realize two out of the three times you've seen this man, he's handed you a fistful of cash?"

"Oh, for heaven's sake, Manny, you make it sound sordid," Ellie said. "It's a simple business arrangement, that's all."

"Sure. And I guess you're naive enough to think this man is going to shell out money like this and be satisfied with a peck on the cheek at the end of the day?"

Ellie frowned. It hadn't occurred to her that Mark would expect anything other than a convincing performance.

"Ellie," Manny continued in her silence, "you already think this man and several other strangers you've encountered are affected by those pills you're taking. Did you ever think it might be dangerous if the pheromones push someone to, you know, take liberties with you?"

"I can take care of myself, Manny," Ellie countered, then she softened. "But I appreciate the concern."

Her roommate touched her arm, his face serious. "I want to meet this guy, to check him out and see if he's safe, okay?"

"You just want to check him out, period." Ellie poked a finger in his side, lightening the mood. "I told you, he's not your type."

Later, when she picked up the developed film from the photo shoot with Mark, Manny's warning of Mark's physical interest resurfaced to send Ellie's heart pounding. She flipped through dozens of photos of his handsome face, and groaned. Not only was the man good-looking, but photogenic, too.

Her breathing became shallow when she came to the photo of Mark shirtless, arms crossed, his eyes haughty from tricking her. Recalling their light, fussy banter, Ellie realized uneasily she could get used to his company. But the memory of the deal they'd struck sobered her immediately. He needed someone his mother would object to, and he'd chosen her for the part. How much clearer could he have made it that he would never be interested in her romantically?

4

"SPARE SOME CHANGE, buddy?" The ragged man's dead tone and tired eyes told Mark he fully expected to take no for an answer.

Mark hesitated outside Ellie's building, then withdrew a five-dollar bill from his wallet and placed it in the man's trembling hand. The man thanked him profusely, then trotted down the street. He wasn't in the habit of giving handouts, but he'd felt a stir when he'd looked into the man's lost eyes. Mark shook his head sadly. His old man had given away and loaned out enough money to save an entire generation. And look where it had gotten Rudy Blackwell.

Mark shook off the somber thoughts of his father and looked around the neat, trendy area. Panhandlers knew Little Five Points inhabitants were liberals, for the most part, with a social conscience and lots of spare change to back it up. Mark knew this because he'd rented an apartment not far from Ellie's building before he'd signed a hefty mortgage and moved north to Dunwoody.

At only eleven-thirty, the sun already hung high and scorching. He pulled a finger around the collar of his golf shirt and felt relieved he'd worn khaki shorts. He'd arrived at Ellie's a few minutes early, but his mother wanted to get to the picnic shelter at Stone Mountain before anyone else so she could prevent relatives from setting green-bean salad next to strawberry pie, or some similar unforgivable act. He chuckled, thinking about Ellie Sutherland and Gloria Blackwell mixing for an entire day. He couldn't imagine the surprises Ellie had in store. This might be the most fun he'd ever had at a family gathering. And it would very likely get his marriage-happy mother off his back.

As he climbed the steps to her second-floor apartment, Mark tried to ignore the anticipation he felt at seeing her again. Many times during the previous sleepless night he'd reminded himself she'd managed to extort a good chunk of cash from him in the one week he'd known her. She was just like the others, he told himself. So why had he tripped twice in his haste to get to her door?

He knocked twice before he heard footsteps approaching. When the door swung open, a tall, handsome blond man stood before him with a questioning look on his face.

"Excuse me," Mark said abruptly. "I must have the wrong apartment."

The man extended his hand in a firm grip. "You must be Mark," he said. "Ellie's almost ready. I'm Manny, Ellie's roommate. Come in."

Mark blinked. A ridiculous stab of jealousy jolted through him. Ellie hadn't mentioned she lived with a man—a very good-looking man, to boot. He followed her roommate through a shallow entryway and halted to stand on the black-and-white kitchen floor, grimacing at the screeching voice that reached his ears. Ellie stood at the stove with headphones on, her back to them, stirring a fragrant concoction in a saucepan and belting out a horrid rendition of Patsy Cline's "Crazy."

Manny turned to him and shrugged apologetically. "It's country this week, next week—who knows?" He walked over and tapped Ellie on the shoulder. She jumped several inches, her hand to her chest, and the shrieking stopped. She saw Mark and smiled, tearing off the headphones.

"Hi," she said, picking up a towel to wipe her hands.

"Hi, yourself," he said, annoyed at the rush of pleasure he felt. "Is that your contribution to the potluck?" he asked, pointing to the gooey liquid in the pan.

Ellie laughed and reached around to untie her frilly cotton apron. A vintage garment, he suspected, noting the pleasantly faded fabric. "That," she said, nodding to the pan, "is twenty-five thousand dollars."

"What?"

"I'm entering a homemade-perfume contest. The entry fee s one hundred dollars, which I'm working off today." She miled at him impishly. "Top prize is twenty-five thousand, nd I want it."

Intrigued, Mark walked over to the pot and sniffed. A sultry lend of musk, fruit and flowers assailed his nostrils. "Hmm," e said, nodding. "Very nice. I've never smelled anything like t. A woman's fragrance, I assume?"

"Of course."

"What's in it?"

"Oh, this and that. Chamomile, marjoram and juniper for elaxation, ylang-ylang as an aphrodi—" She stopped and leared her throat loudly. "Plus vanilla, and a little cocoa."

"It's colorful," he said, noting the muddy brown hue.

"I haven't worked out all the kinks yet, but my idea is to aunch a whole line of perfume products based on foods."

"Pizza perfume?" he asked, teasing.

She smiled. "More like orange marmalade or peach pie."

When she pulled the apron over her head, Mark inhaled harply at the sight of her in a full-skirted, floral minidress nd flat cloth tennis shoes. No bra either, which was not unecoming. She looked all of sixteen. He swallowed. "What lo you call the perfume?"

"I've decided to call it Irresistible You."

Bull's-eye. Mark nodded. "Very appropriate."

She turned off the flame and said, "I see you've met Aanny. Let me grab a couple of things and we'll go." She wept by him in a cloud of homemade fragrance, the pomoms on her socks bouncing up and down as she strode away.

Mark watched her, then turned when he felt Manny watchng him. As the man waved him toward a purple-and-gold elour chair in the tiny living room, Mark again wondered bout his relationship to Ellie. They were both blond, perhaps e was her brother. "Are you related to Ellie?" he asked when hey were seated.

"No," Manny said, tapping a cigarette from a pack and olling it between his fingers. "Ellie and I go way back."

His tone implied intimacy, and Mark didn't really want to delve further.

"She's a great gal," Manny continued. He lit the cigarette inhaled deeply and turned his head to release a stream of white smoke from his mouth. His voice and bearing suggested a challenge.

Mark nodded his agreement, but said nothing. His nose itched ferociously, and he ran a knuckle over it.

"She has men falling all over her."

It seemed like a strange thing for her roommate to say, but Mark smiled amicably. A savage sneeze seized him, and he dragged a handkerchief from his back pocket. Wiping at watery eyes, he sniffed. "I can see why," he finally managed to say.

"Is the smoke bothering you?" Manny asked, cupping his hand over the cigarette.

Mark shook his head. "Smoke never bothers me." On cue he sneezed into the handkerchief three times, each more powerful than the last. "I don't know what's wrong." Mark felt a sudden soft weight land in his lap, and he looked down into the green eyes of a very hairy orange cat. One inhale solved the mystery as Mark dissolved into a sneezing fit, which did nothing to spook the arrogant feline.

"Allergic, huh?" Manny said, stubbing out his cigarette in a nearby ashtray. "Come, Esmerelda." He removed the feline from Mark's knee and disappeared down the same hallway Ellie had taken.

By the time he returned, minus the cat, Mark felt much better.

"Sorry about that," Manny said unconvincingly. "Ellie loves the puss." When he sat down, Manny leaned forward in his chair. "Do you find yourself drawn to her?" he asked.

Mark frowned and drew his shoulders back a couple of inches. "Who?"

"Ellie," Manny said.

"Drawn?"

"Yeah, you know." Manny toyed with another cigarette but didn't light it. "Like *compelled* to be around her?"

Mark glanced from side to side. *Is this guy for real?* "I don't know if I'd use that word exactly," Mark said slowly, "but she does seem to have an effect on me."

Manny's sandy eyebrows shot up and he leaned back, nodding and contemplating. Mark glanced toward the hall. "Ellie?" he called, standing.

To his relief, she appeared with a huge canvas bag over her shoulder. A floppy denim hat nearly hid her cropped wavy hair and made her appear even younger. She smiled and shaved off another couple of years.

"Just how old are you?" he asked.

"Twenty-nine," she said cheerfully. "Did I go overboard?" she asked, looking down at her outfit. Silver earrings brushed the tops of her shoulders. "Your mom will hate it, won't she?" Concern pulled down the corners of her eyes and mouth.

Mark grinned. "Yes."

Ellie grinned, too. "Then let's go." She leaned forward to study his face, undoubtedly red from the sneezing. "Sorry about Esmerelda. She's a hairy thing, isn't she?"

He waved off the incident and reached for her bulging bag, then playfully buckled under its weight. "Let me guess—you brought books to read, didn't you?"

Ellie laughed. "No, just a few necessities for a picnic." She picked up a small bottle from the kitchen counter, shook two pink tablets into her palm and filled a glass with water from the tap.

"Headache?" Mark asked, suddenly concerned.

"Hmm?" Ellie asked. Apprehension crossed her face, then disappeared. "These are just, um...vitamins." She stuck the bottle into the weighted canvas bag. "I have to take them throughout the day," she explained. "Woman stuff," she added in a whisper.

Mark had figured as much and nodded curtly, and he hoped, sympathetically.

When Ellie pulled a huge chocolate layer cake from the fridge, he shot her a questioning look. The last thing he needed was for his mom to think he'd snared a domestic dream.

"Well, I can't go completely empty-handed," she said defensively.

"Okay," Mark relented. "But it'd better not taste *too* good." For a few seconds, he experienced misgivings. What if she did hit it off with his family? If they pestered him to bring her around again, his plan would backfire in his face.

"SO TELL ME, what kind of woman does your mother expect you to marry?" Ellie hoped setting the stage for her performance would soothe her jangled nerves.

Mark pursed his lips and glanced back at the road in front of him. He looked relaxed and athletic in his casual clothes. The muscles in his legs bunched when he shifted gears, sending shocks of awareness through Ellie's body.

"Someone demure and domestic, I suppose. Like her." He smiled wryly. "She thinks I need someone to be a hostess in my home and help me entertain to further my career."

"And you don't?" she asked.

"No," he said flatly.

"Why not?" she persisted.

He sighed. "Because I've seen too many of my friends get rooked into marriage only to find themselves digging out from under a divorce settlement within a couple of years. I worked my tail off to get where I am. I have no intention of starting over."

Ellie sat still, heat burning her neck and cheeks. Mark was convinced that women were fortune seekers. And she'd given him ammunition by lowering his bank account by more than four hundred dollars since she'd met him a week ago. "So," she said, trying to cover her embarrassment, "you've never been married?"

"Nope." Then he shot her a worried glance. "Have you?"

"No," she said quickly, not that it mattered to him anyway.

"Who's Manny?"

For a split second, Ellie felt pleased he even cared, but his concentration on the road and casual tone indicated he was just making conversation. "Just an old friend," she said and

Mark nodded lazily, clearly uninterested. Her heart sank. "Is your mother a widow?"

"Yes," Mark said, frowning slightly. "Dad died three years ago."

"I'm sorry," Ellie said. "Were you close to him?"

"As close as you can be to someone with whom you have nothing in common."

Ellie felt a stirring of kinship. "My father was never around when I was growing up, either."

Mark's low laugh held no humor. "Mine was always around. Couldn't seem to keep a job. He was a great man, but a lousy provider."

"Where do you live?" Ellie asked, searching for firmer ground.

She thought she saw his lips tighten. "Dunwoody," he said.

He didn't have to add "in a big, expensive home." The one word said it all. "Do you have a large yard?" Ellie asked.

Mark glanced at her sideways. "I suppose so."

"Trees?"

"Uh-huh."

"What kinds of plants and flowers?"

Mark shrugged. "The usual stuff—azaleas, forsythia, a few bulb flowers and lots of ground cover. I might build a gazebo this fall."

"That sounds nice," Ellie said, and meant it. Room for a large herb garden was the only thing she yearned for that apartment living couldn't give her.

"I like it," Mark said, his voice tight.

From his manner, Ellie concluded he probably didn't want her discussing domestic things like gardens and homes with his mother.

"How exactly do you want me to act?" Ellie asked. "And what should I talk about?"

Mark smiled again, and she felt a rush of pleasure. "You've got a mom," he said. "You'll know what to say and how to act."

"Don't you feel guilty about lying to your mother?"

Mark shook his head. "I know my mom. It's only when

I'm *not* seeing anyone that she panics and puts me on a guilt trip because she doesn't have grandchildren. The minute I *do* meet someone, she scolds me for neglecting my career and says I've got plenty of time to get married." He relaxed his hands lower on the wheel. "I'd rather not have to stage this little charade, but no one's getting hurt."

Ellie bit her tongue, and a little sliver of disappointment shook her heart. *Speak for yourself, Mark Blackwell.* She'd promised him a wacky performance for his money, but deep down she wished today could be different. It was easy to imagine herself as Mark's girlfriend, on her way to meet his family at a picnic. But, a deal was a deal, and today she'd be everything Mark Blackwell wouldn't want in a partner. The bad thing about it was, she wouldn't have to do much of an acting job. She realized, for the most part, just being herself would be suitably unsuitable.

Gloria Blackwell strutted out to the car exactly as Ellie had envisioned. Buxom and conservatively dressed in a shapeless jumper. Neat hair in a low bun. Plump elbows and arms full of pot holders and steaming casserole dishes.

Gloria gave Ellie's outfit a long glance, then offered a shaky smile. Introductions were cheery and forced. Gloria asked Ellie to move to the back seat of Mark's sedan, citing her perpetual car sickness as the reason she needed the front passenger seat. As Ellie moved to oblige, she heard the woman whisper to Mark, "Isn't she going to miss her prom?"

"Be nice," Mark whispered back.

Ellie smiled wryly. This would be the easiest money she'd ever made. The thought did not ease her conscience.

"Ellie, dear," Gloria asked when they were on their way, "what do you do for a living?"

Ellie hesitated a split second, then said, "I was laid off from a secretarial job a few days ago." She saw Mark frown at the news, then his face cleared, as if in understanding. He winked at Ellie in the mirror. He thought she was making it up to get under his mother's skin!

"So you're unemployed?" his mother asked, her disapproval thinly veiled.

Ellie ground her teeth, but maintained a sweet and pleasant voice. "Well, I'm really an artist, working on my portfolio and doing commissions on the side—like painting your son's portrait."

"An unemployed artist," Gloria chirped. "How interesting." She addressed Ellie by looking at her in the side-door mirror. "My late husband dabbled in paint—it never earned him a penny."

Ellie sat back in her seat, biting off a defensive retort. Gloria Blackwell had disliked her on sight. That fact might have bothered her if she thought this thing with Mark was going anywhere. But since he'd made it clear he wasn't interested in pursuing a relationship, she could relax. So what if his mother pooh-poohed her occupation and clothes? Mark said he wanted to go for shock value. For three hundred and fifty dollars, she'd be Madonna for a day.

"So how did you meet my son?"

"The first time we met, he dumped a cola in my lap and paid me off to avoid a scene."

"And…the next time?" Gloria ventured.

"In the men's room at his law office. Your son has an enormous—"

"I don't think—" Gloria tried to interrupt.

"—bladder," Ellie finished.

Gloria fanned herself. "Do your parents live in Atlanta?"

"No, Florida."

Mark's mother breathed an audible sigh of relief at finding a safe subject. "That's nice. Are they retired?"

"Semi-retired," Ellie said pleasantly. "They run a restaurant."

"How lovely!"

"At a nudist colony."

Gloria gasped and a sudden fit of coughing seized Mark.

Ellie bit back a wry smile.

For the rest of the drive, Gloria conversed with Mark, making general comments about the picnic and who would be there. Ellie guessed Mark's mother would not be directing any more questions her way, so she relaxed into the soft leather seat and listened to the woman's chatter.

"Did I tell you your uncle Jerome will be there? I know you're not fond of him, Marcus, but he *is* your grandmother's only brother. He's married again, did you know?"

Ellie smiled as Mark made a big show of counting off on his fingers. "Is this the fourth wife, or the fifth?"

"Fifth. You know the second Julia was really a gem—we all wish he'd kept her."

"I don't remember his second wife."

"No, I'm talking about Julia, his third wife. His second wife was also Julia, but we didn't care for her. She sniffed all her food before eating it. Always sniffing, it was very annoying. But his third wife, Julia—the second Julia, we always called her—now *there* was a nice girl. Real Southern manners, and a proper wife she was."

Ellie couldn't resist. "If she was such a proper wife, why did he get rid of her?"

Gloria jerked her head around quickly, as if she'd forgotten about their passenger. She adjusted the mirror so she could see Ellie. "I really wouldn't know," she said airily, as if gossiping was beneath her, then adjusted the mirror back with a snap.

"Here we are," Mark said cheerfully, shoving the gearshift into Park and turning off the ignition.

"How am I doing?" Ellie whispered as they walked to the back of the car.

"Great," he said, smiling. "I think she hates you."

Ellie frowned, then nodded agreeably. She was earning her pay, wasn't she?

She spied several shelters within walking distance, but a sign bearing the name "Blackwell" led them to one off to the right and up a small incline.

"I thought this was your mother's family," Ellie said to Mark as they unpacked the food.

He smiled. "It's both, really. Without getting too complicated, my dad and four of his brothers married mom and four of her sisters."

"Is that legal?" Ellie asked.

This time he laughed. "It's legal, but sometimes I don't think it was very smart. All of their children are double first cousins. It makes for a pretty tight-knit group." He pulled a huge cooler from the trunk of his car, and led the way up the path. Gloria hurried ahead, visibly crestfallen that one of her sisters had beaten her to the punch and, having arrived first, was already spreading vinyl tablecloths over the ten or so picnic tables in the shelter.

Within a few minutes, several carloads had arrived, and Ellie's head spun from the names and faces she'd tried to commit to memory. Everyone, including Gloria, seemed impressed with the chocolate cake she'd made. "It's low-fat, too," she said to Gloria.

"Well," harrumphed Mark's mother, giving Ellie a sweeping glance, "not everyone was meant to look like a stick." The cake was thereby relegated to the lowly salad table, to occupy a spot beside a plate of unpopular celery and carrot sticks.

After an hour, Ellie decided to take a break from the adults and mix with Mark's young cousins. Delighted to discover several of them had brought in-line skates, she retrieved hers from her bag and joined them on the paved parking lot, ignoring disparaging looks from Mark's mother. She taught the more experienced skaters a few moves and was soon enjoying herself very much, laughing in spite of the sick feeling building in her stomach. She felt like a fraud, but it was equally disheartening to know that even when she was being herself, Mark's mother disapproved.

As unobtrusively as possible, Ellie watched Mark mix with the odd collection of relatives. The fussy aunts, the crying babies, the joke-telling men were so different from the stoic manner he put on. Ellie wondered how he'd metamorphosed into the polished, articulate executive he'd become. He was obviously everyone's favorite. It was gratifying to see he'd originated from homespun people—good, decent people with simple wants and needs whom he seemed to care about. This was a side of him she hadn't expected to discover, and it caused an unsettling shift in the characteristics she'd assigned to him.

It bothered her, too, that his family was so different from hers. He'd mentioned he was an only child, like Ellie, but Mark's extended family was large and varied, warm and comfortable around each other. She tried to conjure up images of long-forgotten aunts and uncles from faded photographs she'd seen in family albums. Both sets of grandparents had died before she was a toddler. Ellie's mother had been the youngest of her three siblings by nearly a generation—she wasn't close to them at all. Her father had one brother left, living somewhere on the West Coast, she recalled. She wondered how many unknown cousins she had all over the country, and made a mental note to pump her mother for more information the next time they talked on the phone.

She stole a glance at Mark, and felt a zing go through her at the sight of him, his head thrown back, laughing. She envied Mark Blackwell and his rowdy relatives. Ellie sighed. A big, close, loving family was all she'd ever wanted, and all she'd never gotten.

Mark slapped his cousin Mickey on the back, enjoying a shared joke. His gaze slid to Ellie, an annoying habit he'd adopted in the last hour, along with every male relative at the picnic over the age of ten. His smile died and his mouth went dry as she whirled on the skates, causing her skirt to billow alarmingly high.

"Where did you snag *her?*" Mickey whispered hoarsely, admiration tinting his voice.

Mark jerked his head around to find the eyes of his balding, chunky cousin riveted on Ellie. A strange feeling of possessiveness descended over him. "She's an artist and my office commissioned her to do a painting."

"An artist, huh? That explains it."

"That explains what?"

"Why she's not like every corporate female clone I've ever seen you with."

Mark frowned. "What's that supposed to mean?"

"Not that you haven't dated some beauties, cuz," Mickey

hastened to add. "It's just that my tastes lean toward *warm*-blooded creatures." He exhaled heavily. "And that woman is hot."

Mark's frown deepened. He hadn't hired her to be hot. Guilt stabbed him in the gut when he remembered the money he'd paid her. The thought struck him that it might be nice if Ellie Sutherland had accompanied him of her own volition, instead of having to be bribed. Then she could have acted naturally and his family could have fallen in love with her...wait a minute—what was he thinking?

His cousin let out a low whistle through his small teeth. Mark joined him in holding his breath when a particularly risky move revealed every square inch of her rock-hard thighs and the barest glimpse of white cotton undies. Mark licked his lips nervously and Mickey dragged a handkerchief out of his back pocket to mop his forehead.

"I don't think she hit it off with Mom," Mark said carefully, attempting to plant a seed of dissent.

"That settles it," Mickey said, nodding confidently. "Marry her."

Someone rang a bell to signal the meal being served. Ellie removed her skates and rejoined the adults, dutifully giving disappointing, but true, answers to repeated questions from Gloria's sisters about what she did for a living and how she'd met Mark. Mark hovered close by, as if to verify she was doing what he'd asked of her. Every infant at the gathering squalled when she held them, and soon the new mothers were keeping their babies to themselves. Ellie slipped her camera from the bag and snapped two rolls of pictures, the women politely rigid when she focused on them, the men curiously hamming for the camera.

Indeed, it seemed the chilly reception extended to her by the Blackwell women wasn't a feeling shared by the Blackwell men. They buzzed around Ellie continually, laughing and flirting, elbowing appreciation to a silent Mark. Uncle Jerome, the marrying man, shadowed her every move, offering her lively, if suggestive, conversation throughout the afternoon. Even beating the men at horseshoes didn't banish their smiles and winks. When it looked as if the female relatives were about to descend on her with tar and feathers, she rejoined the children. This time, she pulled out her sketchbook and drew caricatures of the ones who could sit still long enough for her to render a pastel drawing. The children gleefully took the sketches to their parents, and before long, an audience had gathered.

The sudden attention made Ellie nervous and she noticed a frown on Mark's face. He wasn't paying her to make a favorable impression. She glanced at her tablet. "One sheet of paper left," she said. "Gloria, how about it?"

Mark's mother suddenly turned shy and blushing, but smiling, she nodded and sat before Ellie, striking a regal pose.

Ellie scanned the woman in front of her for a few seconds. The phrase *queen bee* kept going through her mind. Ellie looked at Mark, who gave her a slight nod. "Go ahead," he seemed to say. "One last nail in the coffin."

Hurriedly, Ellie sketched, hardly looking up. Once finished, she swallowed, amazed at how unkind the picture had turned out. With a bemused smile, Gloria reached for the drawing as everyone gathered around. Instantly her smile dissolved and her face reddened, then she handed it back to Ellie and huffed away amid choruses of laughter from her family.

Mark stepped forward to look at the sketch, a buxom insect with a tiara on her head, wielding a giant-size stinger. He pursed his lips. "Queen bee," he said, studying the drawing with a tight smile. "So true. You're very good."

Ellie watched people drift away to the dessert table and said, "It was hurtful to her, and I should apologize."

Mark shook his head. "You're doing just what I asked you to do," he said, handing the sketch back to her and looking into her eyes. "Everyone got a chuckle out of it. Mom's just not very good at laughing at herself."

"Still, I feel so mean," she said, biting her lower lip.

He extended his hand to her and pulled her up. "Let's get dessert." His first touch sent charges of electricity through her fingers. She quickly withdrew her hand once she got to her feet.

When everyone discovered Ellie's cake was low-fat, most of the women relented and served themselves portions ranging from polite to generous. Uncle Jerome even teased Gloria into having a chunk, pointing out it wouldn't hurt her to start counting her fat grams. Gloria begrudgingly ate every crumb. The men deferred to more fattening fare. Mark declined, saying he wasn't big on sweets, and Ellie declined as well so someone else could have the remaining piece. To her surprise, it was Gloria.

"Are you sure this is low in fat?" she asked Ellie, shoveling in the second piece. "It's surprisingly good."

Ellie beamed, glad she would leave with one redeeming mark. "The guy I live with gave me the recipe." When she saw Gloria's eyes widen in response to the remark about her roommate, Ellie hurried on, "This is the first time I've made it. I'm glad it's as good as he said it would be."

"You know," Gloria said thickly through a mouthful, "Marcus needs a good cook in his kitchen."

Ellie's smile froze, wondering if Mark had overheard the comment. She nodded woodenly, surprised at the concession his mother had made, but more surprised at how good the idea sounded, her cooking in Mark's kitchen. Of course, they'd have to eat chocolate cake every night since it was the first and only thing she'd ever made that had turned out well enough to actually serve. Avoiding Mark's eyes, Ellie enjoyed the slight lifting of her heart.

About halfway through the hokey-pokey, the Blackwell women started dropping like flies. Clutching their stomachs, they ran for the nearest bathroom, several yards away. Gloria seemed to be the most violently ill. When they emerged an hour later, wiping sweat from their clammy foreheads, they'd determined the culprit must be Ellie's cake since no one else had been afflicted.

White as a sheet and mad as a hornet, Gloria demanded, "What did you put in that cake?"

Ellie backed up a step and tried to keep the shakiness out of her voice. "The normal stuff—flour, eggs, cocoa, prune juice—"

"Prune juice?" Gloria screeched. "Who puts prune juice in chocolate cake?"

"It replaces the oil and m-makes the cake low f-fat," Ellie stammered.

"How much did you put in?" Gloria asked, her eyes bulging.

"A b-bottle of concentrated—" She stopped at the horrified looks around her. "A s-small bottle," she added weakly, holding up her thumb and index finger.

"A whole bottle? Lord, we'll be purging for a week—" Gloria stopped, grabbed her stomach and trotted back up the hill to the rest room, followed by six others.

Ellie closed her eyes and took a deep breath. When she opened them, Mark stood before her, a wry smile on his face. "That really wasn't necessary, Ellie—" he took her hand "—but it certainly cinched you a spot on my mother's least-likely-to-be-a-good-daughter-in-law list."

Her senses leaped when he touched her, her mouth instantly parched. She swallowed miserably. He'd never believe her if she told him none of it had been planned. Ellie fought back tears of frustration.

This day had proved one thing to her. She was inherently wrong for Mark Blackwell.

MARK SWUNG his glance from the road ahead to Ellie's profile and tried to guess what she was thinking. The day was an unqualified success as far as his original plan was concerned, but he hadn't counted on his feelings shifting somewhere between the time he'd picked her up and the time he dropped her off. Away from her, he seemed able to logically dismiss her. But once in her presence, some undefined feeling took control.

"Your pictures turned out well," she said, breaking the silence and, thankfully, his train of thought.

"Did they?"

"Yes." She still stared straight ahead, her voice unreadable. "I think the dark gold background will be the best, if that's okay with you."

"You're the artist," he said.

"Yes, and I'm very proud of what I do," she said, a note of defensiveness in her voice.

"As well you should be," he said quickly, once again speaking to her profile. Suddenly he remembered the disparaging remark he'd made about her being an artist when she first came to his office. And, the raised eyebrows and rolling eyes of his mother and her sisters had not escaped him today. Apparently, they hadn't escaped Ellie, either. "I admire your talent," he said sincerely.

She didn't respond, but her head shifted slightly toward him.

"It was a nice day," he said lightly.

Ellie's dry laugh rang out. "Sure it was," she said miserably. "I gave enemas to your mother and all of your aunts."

"Most of them have been constipated all their lives." He chuckled, but at the look on Ellie's face, he bit his lip to stem his laughter. "It's okay—no one was hurt." Actually, he couldn't remember enjoying a family gathering more than he had today. His family's bout with diarrhea aside, he'd enjoyed watching Ellie skate and mix with his young cousins. And cut up with his uncles. And her drawing ability was truly special. She was a very unusual woman, and damned attractive, at that. Another peek at her in the semidarkness of the car revealed a long expanse of lean, tanned leg. His right hand itched to reach over and rub the smooth length of skin.

"When can you sit for your portrait again?" she asked.

"How about Saturday morning? That is," he added quickly, "if you don't mind spending another Saturday with me." He held his breath for her response. Could he wait another six days to see Ellie again?

"Saturday morning is fine," she said, finally swinging her head around to meet his gaze.

"Fine," he said, feeling the breath leave his lungs. God, she was beautiful. "Fine," he heard himself repeat. His groin tightened uncomfortably and he dragged his eyes away from hers. Her apartment building loomed ahead on the left.

"Thanks," Ellie said quickly, hopping out as soon as he pulled to a stop.

"Wait," he said to the closed door. He cut the ignition and jumped out of the car. "Wait," he called, and she turned back struggling under the weight of that ridiculous bag. "I'll walk you to your door." He strode toward her, his knees suddenly rubbery. Would she let him kiss her? Would a kiss be appropriate under the circumstances? And when was the last time he had ever worried about whether or not to kiss a woman good-night?

She waited until he'd caught up and taken her bag, but remained a couple of steps ahead of him, walking into the apartment building and up to her door on the second floor.

"Thanks," she said, sounding a little breathless.

"You did me the favor," he said, referring to the picnic.

She smiled. "I meant, thanks for walking up with me. It wasn't necessary, but nice."

He could barely see her eyes for the brim of her hat, which sat slightly askew. New freckles glowed across her cheeks from the afternoon's sunshine. Her lips held the frosty remnants of pink lipstick long since faded. She hadn't bothered to renew it. How refreshing to be with a woman who was content to be her natural self sometimes. He wet his lips. "Ellie?"

She raised wide, innocent eyes to his. "Yes?" She didn't have a clue he wanted to kiss her. And why should she? He'd hired her to go on a picnic with him. The whole arrangement seemed very impersonal at the moment. Did he dare?

"Ellie?" he repeated.

"What is it, Mark?" she asked, her head slightly angled.

"This," he breathed, lowering his mouth to hers. Her lips were silken, parting to accept his fully, her tongue tentatively offered. Desire shot through his body. He dropped the canvas bag with a loud thud and took her into his arms to draw her deeper into the kiss. Suddenly, the apartment door swung open.

Mark and Ellie parted and turned their heads to see a questioning Manny, holding a half-eaten apple. "I heard a thump," ıe explained, leaning on the door frame and taking a large ›ite.

Mark straightened. *What is the deal with this roommate nan, anyway?*

Everyone stared at everyone else, the silence broken only ›y Manny's loud chewing. After a few seconds, Mark cleared ıis throat. "Well, I'd better be going."

Manny reached inside the door to retrieve a light jacket rom a hook. "I was on my way out myself—just wanted to nake sure you got home safely, El." He flashed her a tight mile. "I'll walk out with Mr. Blackwell." He took a last bite ›ut of the apple for punctuation and tossed it into a trash can ›eside the door. Then he stepped squarely between them in he hall, struggling into his jacket with exaggerated movenents that obstructed Mark's view of Ellie.

Mark frowned slightly, then said, "I'll see you Saturday, Ellie." He peeked around Manny's breadth as the man took ıis time pulling on the jacket. Ellie said nothing, but he saw—eproachfulness?—flicker in her eyes. Had his kiss been unvelcome? It hadn't seemed so, but then again she hadn't ounted on her roommate/boyfriend/whatever catching them.

Mark walked side by side with Manny down the stairs and ›ut into the dusk. They stopped on the sidewalk and Mark vithdrew his car keys. "So," he said casually, "what's your elationship with Ellie?" He pressed a button on his key ring ınd his car interior light came on a few feet away. Mark swung ıis attention back to her roommate.

Manny stood with his hands in his jacket pockets, studying Mark silently with narrowed eyes. Finally, the tall blond man poke quietly, "Ellie means more to me than anyone else in his world. Don't break her heart, mister." With that, he turned ınd walked away, pulling a cigarette from his pocket and poking it in his mouth.

Driving away, Mark decided it had been one of the most ınsettling days of his life. The picnic had been unexpectedly enjoyable, and Ellie's good-night kiss unexpectedly flammable. Feelings nagged at him, annoying him like radio static. Just exactly what did Ellie Sutherland mean to him, other than a guaranteed end to his orderly life?

5

"YOU DIDN'T!" Manny looked horrified.

"I did." Ellie nodded solemnly, slathering jelly on a plain bagel. Breakfast was the first chance they'd had to talk. "You should have seen those big women running for the john. And we had to stop three times on the way home for his mom to go."

"I always said you were going to poison someone with your cooking one of these days," he chided. "You've got to remember, preparing food is not the same as whipping up one of your perfume batches."

Ellie brightened. "Which reminds me, I'm sending a vial of Irresistible You to the contest today." She pointed to a small bottle of reddish-brown liquid beside a gummy saucepan. The recipe I came up with yesterday turned out just right, after all."

Manny shook his head. "You can kiss that hundred-dollar entry fee goodbye. It's a scam, El."

"No, it isn't," she insisted. "I know someone whose cousin's girlfriend won the contest two years ago. And my proposal for a line of fragrances is a great idea."

"Who wants to go around smelling like food?"

"For your information, studies show men are more turned on by the smell of pumpkin pie than by most expensive store-bought fragrances."

"Makes you wonder what Betty Crocker wears under her apron, eh?"

"Go ahead, make fun, but I'll get the last laugh. That twenty-five grand is mine." She rubbed her thumb against her fingers to emphasize her quest for big money.

"You'd better hope so," he said. "It doesn't sound as if you're in danger of marrying into the Blackwell bank account."

Ellie stiffened. "Very funny."

"Hey," he said, laughing gently, "I was kidding, okay? Don't look so wounded. I thought you weren't impressed with this guy."

"I'm not." Ellie studied Esmerelda's paw, refusing to look at her roommate. "He's too much like my father, you know...corporate. I want a man who worships the ground I walk on, who isn't tied to his desk, who would play hooky just to spend the day with his kids. My mother never had that, but I intend to, one of these days."

Manny groaned. "Despite your wish list, you've fallen for him, haven't you?"

Ellie opened her mouth, but Manny held up his hands to ward off her protest. "Before you say anything, Ellie, let's look at this in black and white. The guy hired you to make a bad impression on his family—this is not the sign of a marrying man. Why on earth would you put yourself through the agony of going after someone who's made it perfectly clear he doesn't want to be caught?"

Ellie tried to speak, but once again he stopped her. "But," he said in a singsongy voice, "it's nothing to me." Manny stooped to pick up the cat. "Not to change the subject, but we have other problems more imminent than your love life. Have you noticed anything different about Esmerelda?"

"No," Ellie murmured, popping the pinks pills into her mouth with a grapefruit-juice chaser. "Why do you ask?"

"Here," he said, handing Ellie the furry package.

She abandoned her glass to juggle the struggling feline. "She's heavier," Ellie said immediately, shifting the cat slightly for confirmation. "We should have put you on a diet weeks ago," she said, snuggling the cat's face to her own.

"We should have put her on a *leash,*" Manny amended, arms crossed and lips tight.

"What do you mean?"

"Esmerelda is knocked up."

Ellie's eyes widened. "Kittens? Are you sure?" She held the cat up to scrutinize her rounded tummy, grinning. "It must've happened on one of those days she escaped."

"Must have," Manny chirped. "You realize, don't you, this means your cat has a better sex life than you do?"

She shot him an exasperated look. "Oh, Manny, do you have to be so…so…"

"The word is *truthful,*" he supplied. He plucked a piece of paper from the counter and waved it in front of her. "It gets worse. This was under our door when I got up this morning."

Ellie reached for the paper and gasped at the words in large print across the top of the page. "Eviction notice? Why?" She began reading the sheet in earnest, but Manny cut in.

"It's the cat, El. She got out one too many times and someone complained. According to the notice, we have one week to find a home for her or we'll have to find a new home for ourselves."

"I'll find someone to take her in," she said, gently setting Esmerelda on the floor, then reaching for the phone.

Two hours later Ellie had called every person in both her address book and Manny's, but no one could shelter her precious cat. She sighed, explaining to Manny, "Denise has a new baby, the Worths have a dog, and Robin just bought a bird. Everyone else already has too many cats or kids, or lives in a no-pet unit." Ellie pulled Esmerelda to her and relished the deep purr of the mother-to-be. "What am I going to do?"

"YOUR MOTHER CALLED TWICE," Monica said, handing Mark the message sheets. "She asked me to tell you to call her back as soon as you get a minute."

Mark nodded absently and laid the notes aside.

Looking over his shoulder, Monica asked, "What's so important about Saturday?"

Mark glanced up at her and frowned in confusion.

She pointed to his calendar. "It's circled. Do I need to add something to my schedule?"

Mark realized with a start he'd circled the day while thinking about Ellie. "No," he said quickly, then added, "just another sitting for the portrait."

Monica's left eyebrow rose a fraction and she smiled. "Oh, yes, the cute little painter. Are sparks still flying between the two of you?"

He feigned innocence. "What do you mean?"

Monica brought her steno pad to her chest and crossed her arms. "What I mean is, when she came to meet you that first day, you were at each other's throats. I haven't mentioned it, but you two have got me curious."

Mark felt his neck grow moist beneath his collar. "A simple misunderstanding in a delicatessen, that's all."

His assistant leaned forward slightly, as if eager for more details, but Mark picked up a memo on his desk and began reading to signal an end to the subject. Monica took the hint and walked toward the door.

"Hey," his partner Patrick said as he strolled in after a perfunctory knock.

"Hey, yourself."

"Clear your calendar Friday evening."

"Okay. Mind telling me why?"

"Lucy's organizing a dinner party and my instructions are to make sure you come." He grinned at Mark apologetically. "Can you scrounge up a date? Ivan will be there, too," he added in explanation.

Ellie's face rose to float in Mark's mind, but he squashed down the image. "Is an escort mandatory?"

Patrick shrugged. "I have my orders." He turned to leave Mark's office and added over his shoulder, "Come stag at your own risk."

"It might be safer than the alternative," Mark muttered as Ellie's face stubbornly reappeared to taunt him. Absurdly happy for a reason to call her, his fingers itched to punch her number. Then, furious with himself, he deliberately dialed Valerie's work number instead. He'd managed to keep from getting emotionally involved with a woman for this long, and he wasn't about to start with someone who was obviously so wrong for him.

But when Valerie responded with such clinging enthusiasm at the sound of his voice, he winced and manufactured a vague excuse for calling. Within seconds of hanging up, his traitorous fingers dialed Ellie's number from memory. Instantly nervous, he wondered if he'd have to bribe her again, or if she'd go freely this time. Too late, the thought surfaced that she might feel obligated to buy a new dress. And he suspected she couldn't afford it.

"Hello." She sounded breathless, and he imagined her in her work apron, wiping her hands after working on some creative project.

"Hi, it's Mark," he said, then added, "Blackwell."

"Oh, hi," she said with a slight question in her voice.

Mark felt awkward and fished for conversation. "Are you busy?"

"As a matter of fact, I was preparing the canvas for your portrait." Animation exuded from her voice. He liked the musical quality of it, not throaty and superficial like most of the women he knew.

"I don't have a clue as to what that entails. Is it difficult?"

Ellie laughed lightly, a tinkling sound. "No, I tack canvas over a wooden frame, then paint over it with gesso, a white substance that makes the canvas stiff when it dries."

"Ah, I see," Mark murmured.

The silence stretched for thirty seconds, then they both started talking at once.

"What's up—"

"The reason I called—"

They both laughed and then Mark started again. "The reason I called is to see if you're busy Friday night. I'm in another bind—are you up for a dinner party at the home of one of my partners?"

Ellie's heart had just stopped thudding from the initial shock of hearing his voice. Now it began pounding anew, followed by a sharp barb of disappointment. Apparently, he needed another date for hire. Or maybe not. Maybe this would be a real date. "I, uh, that is...what did you have in mind?"

Mark hesitated for an instant. "Same terms as before?"

Ellie's heart sank, then she panicked. Oh, God, did he think she was trying to wangle a higher price? "Look," she said finally, "I'm caught up on all my bills, so thanks, but I really don't need... Wait a minute." Her mind raced furiously. "How about a business proposition?"

"Go on." This time, *he* sounded cautious.

"My cat needs a home for a few weeks."

"Impossible," he began. "I'm allergic—"

"And I'm desperate," Ellie interrupted, pleading. "She's pregnant and my landlord won't let me keep her—"

"I really can't—"

"Please? Just until the kittens are born and I find homes for them? That's only four or five weeks—eight at the most. Once Esmerelda's gone, he'll get off my back. Then I'll be able to sneak her in again later."

Mark exhaled heavily. "I really can't...believe I'm doing this," he finished, with wonder in his voice. "Okay, it's a deal."

Ellie grinned into the phone. "Great! I'll get a cab to your house Friday night and bring Esmerelda with me." She scribbled down the address. "What should I wear?"

"I'll have something sent over," he said, surprising her.

"I *do* have clothes, *Mr.* Blackwell."

"Why is everything an argument with you? Let me do this, okay?"

He obviously didn't trust her judgment. Or perhaps he wanted her to make another bad impression. Either way, the ball bounced in his court. "Okay," she agreed hesitantly.

"I'll see you Friday," he said, then hung up.

Ellie sat holding the phone and listened to the dial tone. Her scalp tingled. Every day it seemed her life became more enmeshed with Mark Blackwell's. The memory of his kiss had kept her up late last night. She felt warm now just remembering how she'd pulled the length of green velvet from the foot of her bed and slept with it cuddled against her cheek.

She touched her lips, her mouth watering at the thought of his taste. For a brief moment, he'd pulled her to him and she'd felt his arousal for her. Desire stabbed her even now and she allowed herself the luxury of wondering what it would be like to lie beneath him. She knew the pheromones were getting to him—he'd probably bed her willingly enough, she mused. But was her heart durable enough to withstand the letdown once the chemical reaction fizzled out?

The following day, Tuesday, marked exactly one week since Ellie had begun taking the pills. She dutifully collected her journal and walked the few blocks to the clinic.

The unadorned white two-story building squatted on Parish Street between a parking garage and a vintage clothing store. Ellie waited politely while two women entered the door in front of her, wrinkling her nose appreciatively when the smell of paint wafted out. The old structure was getting a face-lift.

Two giant stepladders flanked the wide entryway, supporting slow painters with big paint buckets and tiny brushes. Ellie tilted her head back to check their pace and progress. They'd be there at least a decade, she decided, then turned toward the empty waiting room, relieved she wouldn't have to wait.

A cold, slimy dollop of something plopped onto her head. Ellie closed her eyes and lifted her shoulders in a deep shrug, instinctively wanting to touch the stuff oozing down behind both ears, but already knowing it was off-white wall paint.

"Sorry," came a muffled voice many feet above her. "Nice buns, though."

"Thanks," Ellie mumbled without looking up.

Thirty minutes later she sourly joined a large cluster of people waiting to speak to the harried receptionist standing behind the tall white counter. The clinic was a busy little place. Apparently, a crowd had arrived during her attempt to remove most of the paint from her hair in the rusty old bathroom.

After a long wait, she was directed to one of the cracking vinyl-upholstered chairs lining the perimeter of the waiting room. Ellie passed the time leafing through an ancient copy of *Museum Art,* her hair dripping milky water on the curled pages.

At last her name was called, and she followed a gray-haired, stocky, somber-faced woman to a tiny closet of a room. "I'm

Freda," the woman said defensively, as if Ellie was going to make something of it.

She didn't. "Pleased to meet you."

Freda looked more like a prison guard than a clinical assistant. After a perfunctory glance over her chart, the woman snatched Ellie's journal and perused the contents with tight lips. After a few moments, her eyes swung up to meet Ellie's. "Impressive," the woman muttered. "All true?"

Ellie nodded patiently.

"Are you taking the pills exactly as directed?"

"Yes."

"Any physical symptoms? Changes in energy level or diet?"

Ellie thought for a moment. "My concentration seems diminished, and my appetite has been depressed." She grinned and patted her stomach. "I've lost two pounds."

"How about your exercise level?"

Ellie shook her head. "About average—no change."

The woman noted Ellie's answers on a form. "Have you become sexually active with any of the men you've mentioned in the journal?"

Ellie squirmed. "No."

"Have you developed an emotional attachment to any of them?" She skimmed the last journal page with her index finger. "I see the name Mark mentioned quite often." She peered over her glasses at Ellie.

Clearing her throat, Ellie said, "N-no. Well, maybe."

"I don't have a checkbox for 'maybe,'" said Freda. "Do you like the man or don't you?"

"Yes, I do."

"And do you have reason to think he likes you?"

"I'm not sure *like* is the right word. He looks at me in this certain way…"

"Do you feel the pheromone pills have in any way influenced this, er, watchfulness?"

"Yes, I do."

"In what way?"

Ellie hesitated, then tried to put the situation in words. "He seems to be attracted to me, but confused by it all—like he doesn't understand why he would be. I've seen him shake his head as if trying to clear it. He told my roommate I have 'an effect' on him. And, he and other men keep asking me what kind of perfume I'm wearing. I think I'm emitting some kind of odor."

Freda leaned toward her, sniffed mightily, then shrugged. "Hmm." She scribbled notes on the form and turned it over. "Keep omitting any commercial body fragrances like we instructed. Here's a new supply of pills, and your payment for the week." She pushed the items toward Ellie and resumed writing.

"I mean, it's nothing serious," Ellie rambled. "I wouldn't even call it a relationship, really. It would never work between us because he's allergic to my cat and his mother hates me. Of course, I did ruin her family reunion, but that was purely by accident. Besides, if he ever settles down, it'll be with some classy woman, not an unemployed artist. No, it would never work, not in a million years." Ellie frowned at the woman's silence. "Any advice?" she asked.

Freda didn't bother to look up. "Practice safe sex."

MANNY LET OUT a long whistle. "Damn, you look good, girl."

Ellie grinned and smoothed a hand over the short black crepe dress. "Think so?" A froth of pearl-studded cream chiffon floated around the low neckline and spilled over her shoulders. The formfitting dress would have been an impossibility two pounds ago.

"Fabulous," Manny said cloyingly, then he frowned. "If only we wore the same size."

"I'll let you borrow the earrings," she promised, fastening the dangling pearls.

"He must have spent a mint," he said, picking up the Parmond's garment bag.

Ellie nodded. "What are you doing tonight?"

"I have to do an early show, then Joan's picking me up. We're going to swing by a friend's house for cocktails, then downtown for some real fun. By the way, El, she feels terrible for having to let you go.''

She shrugged. ''It was just a job. So tell me, does Joan like men or women?''

''Neither, as far as I can tell—or maybe both. You know how outrageous Joan can be—I think she likes to keep everyone guessing.''

''Well, tell her hello for me, and that the commission is going well. Will you help me gather Esmerelda's things? The cab should be here any minute.''

The cabbie appeared daunted when he saw the cat and all her feline paraphernalia, but when Ellie smiled at him, he softened and began loading the trunk of the car.

'''Bye, Cinderella,'' Manny said to Ellie before she stepped into the back seat. ''Have a good time at the party. But remember to take your pills or you'll turn into my cousin Betty at midnight.''

ELLIE HAD TRIED to visualize Mark's house, but two blocks away from his address, she realized his home would surpass all her expectations. The cabbie pulled up to a two-story, taupe-colored stucco house with elaborate arches and pale cornerstones. The sloping yard was a paradise, the lawn all but completely sacrificed to tall trees, enormous mulch beds and lush leafy plants. Mounds of blooms flowed downhill. A fountain of stacked stone bubbled a stream of water, which fed an aquamarine goldfish pond. Ellie had never seen a more beautiful sight.

''Are you sure this is the place?'' she breathed.

''Sure as shootin'.'' The driver nodded. ''Nice spread, eh? Friend of yours?''

''Yes,'' she said absently, unable to take her eyes from the house.

''Some guys have all the luck,'' he said dismally. ''But if you get bored with Richie Rich, my name's Cal, and I get off at ten.'' He swung out of the cab and opened her door before she had a chance to respond.

The front door of the house opened. Mark came out and

descended the steps to the walkway. He wore dark slacks, a crisp off-white shirt and a mustard-colored tie. He looked absolutely devastating. Ellie alighted from the cab and smiled toward him. She could detect the clean scent of his cologne as he neared her. Esmerelda struggled for release to inspect the fish, but Ellie held on tight. "Hi," she said.

"Hi." He smiled, and held his hands at his sides, swinging them slightly as if not knowing what to do next.

"Nice house."

"Thanks. Nice dress."

"Thanks."

"Nice bill," the cabbie spoke up, motioning to Mark.

Mark reached for his wallet and counted off several bills, folded them, then handed them to the man.

The cabbie thanked him and opened the trunk. Mark's eyebrows shot up. "What's all this?"

Ellie stepped to the back of the car. "Esmerelda's things."

Mark passed a hand over his face. "You've got to be kidding."

"No," Ellie said, pointing. "Her bed, litter box, kitty litter, food bowl, water bowl, food, brush, play gym, scratch pole, toys, videos—"

"Videos?"

"Sure—one shows birds flying around, the other is of fish swimming and splashing. They keep her entertained for hours."

Mark nodded and pursed his lips. "I see."

The cabbie started pulling things out and setting them on the sidewalk.

"I wrote down her schedule for you." Ellie pulled a sheet of paper from her tiny evening bag. "She's got a bladder infection right now, so you'll need to give her medication once a day." She looked up and recognized impatience on Mark's face. Suddenly he sneezed violently. "We can go over this later," she said with a weak smile, refolding the sheet.

While Mark made several trips to bring in the cat's accessories, Ellie stood in the two-story slate foyer of his home and stretched her neck to see as much as possible from her vantage point. The open layout and cool colors stole her breath. A large living room stretched to her left, an expansive dining room to her right. His furniture was fairly traditional in design, but light fabrics and colors lifted and extended the rooms.

"Wow," Ellie said out loud. If she hadn't been sure before that she and Mark Blackwell existed in different worlds, she was convinced now.

Esmerelda yowled and jumped from Ellie's arms, bounding up the stairs. "Esmerelda!" she yelled, then took off after her.

When Mark entered the house with the last armload, he found the foyer empty. "Ellie," he called, setting the things down on the stairs. He sneezed, and pulled a handkerchief from his pocket to blow his nose. "This is unbelievable," he muttered. "Why did I agree to this?" An implausible answer skated across his mind, but he dismissed it.

When she didn't respond, he walked around the first floor, thinking she might have gone to the bathroom. When he found the door to the downstairs bath ajar, however, he assumed she'd gone upstairs to look around. One of the things that had impressed him the most when she'd asked about his home was that she'd seemed much more interested in his yard than in the grandeur of the house. Mark felt a slight pang of disappointment that she'd been so anxious to check out his digs that she'd helped herself to a tour.

He climbed the stairs, calling her name as he walked room to room. He heard a muffled sound coming from his bedroom and frowned. Not that he hadn't entertained ideas of Ellie seeing the inside of his bedroom, but her forwardness annoyed him slightly.

When he entered his bedroom, he covered his mouth to smother a chuckle, then decided she couldn't hear him, so he laughed out loud, anyway. Ellie Sutherland's very fine-looking rear end stuck straight up in the air, the points of her high heels following suit. He'd pictured her in his bed many times, but never under it. Her head and shoulders were hidden beneath the dust ruffle of his black bed, and she seemed to be saying something, he surmised, to the cat.

After enjoying a full minute of the delectable view, he spoke loudly. "Ellie?"

She raised her head quickly and he heard bone collide with metal. "Darnit!" she yelled, her voice still muffled by all the fabric surrounding her.

Mark laughed again, this time more quietly.

She inched her way backward, out from under the bed, and Mark felt his groin tighten as her hips tested the strength of the dress's seams. He couldn't remember when he'd ever found a woman more appealing than at that very moment.

Her head appeared, her hair wonderfully mussed. She dragged her fingers through it and stood awkwardly, brushing the front of her dress. "I'm sorry," she said. "Esmerelda jumped out of my arms and ran up here and under your bed. I didn't mean to snoop." She chewed on her bottom lip, her glorious blue eyes wide with worry. "I think she's scared."

Her beauty slammed into him with enough power to stagger his senses. *I think I know how the cat feels.* "I'll put her things in the guest room down the hall. Will she come out and look for her bed later?"

Ellie nodded. "Probably."

"Then leave her. How about a drink before we go?"

Ellie smiled at him and his breath caught. "Can I use your bathroom for some repair work first?"

"Sure." He pointed to the master bath. "I'll meet you downstairs."

Ellie took a few seconds to glance around his bedroom, impressed at the sheer size of the bed. King-size and sleekly modern, the elevated bed reigned over a huge room lit by a bay window encompassing an entire wall.

She walked into the spacious bathroom and flipped on the light. "Mmm," she murmured, taking in the tiled floor and large sunken tub. Gold fixtures winked at her from the long double vanity and porcelain sinks. The fragrance of his aftershave lingered. A razor drained on a folded hand towel. Frosted doors encased a shower large enough for a quartet. She could picture Mark showering, soap running down his slick body. She bit her bottom lip and shook her head at th image, then turned to fix her hair.

She gasped at her reflection. Besides her explosive hair, th expensive dress he'd bought her was covered with long ca hairs and carpet fibers. And her lipstick smeared down th corner of her mouth. She groaned, opening her purse and spil ing its contents across the counter in her haste. Ellie tugged brush through her hair, yelping when it skated over the lum fast forming from her encounter with the bed rail. Tears c frustration gathered in her eyes.

"Look at you," she said miserably. "You're a nobody gc ing nowhere. What business do you have falling in love wit Mark Blackwell?" Gasping at her own words, Ellie covere her mouth with her hand. Taking a shaky deep breath, sh straightened her shoulders, and set about making herself pre sentable again. All the while, she hummed to herself, takin great pains not to talk to the crazy woman in the mirror.

6

LLIE FELT SPARKLY from the two rum drinks she'd downed › alleviate her nervousness before they left. Too late, she ·alized she should have had a nonalcoholic beer with Mark. he could feel her body pulling toward him in the darkness f the car. His cologne, the soothing music, the special dress, l of it combined to make her feel languid and sexy. A shiver f premonition traveled the nape of her neck and she trembled. rying to shake the feeling, she turned to Mark as they exited ıe expressway and said, "Any last-minute instructions?"

Mark looked at her, eyebrows lifted and said, "Such as?"

Ellie shrugged. "Such as, is there anybody in particular I'm ıpposed to make dislike me?"

Mark stared at her for a moment, then quietly said, "No, ıst be yourself."

A pretty scary prospect in itself, she thought. "Will your artners be there?"

Mark nodded. "Ray Ivan will be the one with the pipe. His 'ife passed away only a year ago, so I suspect he'll be alone. 'he other partners and their wives will be there, and various uests, I suppose."

When he maneuvered the sedan into a luxurious neighbor-ood, Ellie's shoulders tensed.

"Hey," he said, reaching over to cover her hand with his. 'Relax. You look wonderful."

His touch electrified her hand. Ellie swelled under his raise. "Any woman would in this dress."

He pulled the car behind a long string of vehicles in a semi-ark driveway, then cut the engine. He unfastened his seat belt, ırned toward her and leaned forward until his lips were mere inches from her face. "Not true," he said, then dipped h head to sweep a quick kiss on her jawbone. "Trust me." H voice reverberated in her ear, flaming her senses. Ellie swa lowed hard at the rush of desire flooding her body.

Mark looked into her eyes. "We were rudely interrupte last weekend outside your door," he whispered.

Ellie tried to smile. "Oh, that M-Manny. He's always look ing out f-for me."

He smiled, his eyes crinkling at the corners. "You're n scared of me, are you?"

Terrified. "N-no, of course not. That's not what I meant—

He silenced her words with his mouth, his lips hungril descending upon hers. Her throat constricted for want c much-needed moisture and oxygen, then she finally remem bered to breathe. His tongue parlayed hers in a sensual battl she gladly forfeited. He twined his hands firmly around he waist, she lifted her arms to his neck and wrested sideways t deepen the embrace.

Something restrained her, prevented her from meeting hi fully. She reached down to fumble with the seat belt and snapped loose, tangling in his arms, then hers as they struggle to free themselves. Gasping for breath, they dived at eac other again. This time Mark lifted her, putting his hands be neath her hips to pull her up and against his chest. She coul sense his mounting frustration at the awkward angle. Suddenl he pulled her over the low console to straddle his lap. Her ha brushed the ceiling of the car and the steering wheel presse into her back as she settled around his arousal, her dress hike up to expose the garter belt she wore. Somewhere along th way she'd lost her shoes, but she didn't care. All that mattere was Mark Blackwell touching her, wanting her.

Mark thought he might climax on the spot when his hand discovered the snaps of her garter belt. This woman was kill ing him. "Ellie," he whispered against her neck. She arche her breasts against his chin and he buried his face in her cleav age. She rained kisses over his forehead as she wrapped he arms around his head to pull him closer. He bit lightly at he hardened nipples through the fabric of her dress and bra. Hi hands rode her waist, pushing her down on his arousal. The blood pounded in his brain as it exited, rushing to his midsection. Her breathing rasped as ragged as his as she moaned her pleasure.

"Hey!" a voice shouted outside the window. Mark jerked his head up and panic seized him. One glance confirmed his worst fear. Ray Ivan stood there, crouched and peering into the window. "Blackwell? Is that you? Get a room, son!" Then his partner turned and walked toward their host's home.

They were still for a few seconds as the realization of their indiscretion sunk in. Mark laid his head back and groaned. His arousal wilted. He opened his eyes and looked into Ellie's, wide with concern.

"That was bad, wasn't it?" she asked, biting her lip.

Mark stared at her for a few seconds, then burst out laughing at the incongruity of the situation. And the more he laughed, the harder he laughed. Soon, Ellie joined him as she climbed from his lap and fell into her own seat.

Slapping her knee, Ellie laughed and laughed, until she realized Mark had fallen silent. Looking at his suddenly somber profile, she emitted a final, weak giggle, then cleared her throat.

"What is it about you?" he asked, still staring straight ahead. His rumpled hair and slack mouth were in startling contrast to his dressy attire and normally regal bearing.

Uneasiness crept over Ellie as she fished for her shoes under the seat. "What do you mean?"

He looked over at her with an exasperated expression. "I mean, you drive me to do crazy things like make out in the front seat of my car at a business dinner!"

Anger flashed through Ellie and she pointed her index finger at him. "I didn't exactly fly over there and land on your lap, buster!"

He turned back to stare ahead, then raised his hands in a questioning gesture. "I'm a normal, red-blooded guy, but I've never done anything this stupid before." He spoke quietly, as if to himself, his hands animated. "After all these years of busting my butt and keeping my nose clean, my partner now thinks I'm Mr. Happy Pants."

Ellie sat up, and snapped open her purse to retrieve a comb. The pheromone pills fell into her lap, and she froze. She straightened her dress and asked, "Are we still going in?"

"If you're up to it, I am. I'm sorry I put you in this situation—"

"It's all right, Mark," Ellie assured him guiltily. If not for those magic pills of hers, the whole incident would never have happened. "Let's just make the best of it."

"You're right," he said, adjusting his tie. "It'll look worse if we don't go in. Thanks for being a sport."

They spent a few minutes righting their clothes, then stepped out into the cool early-June night air. Ellie took several deep breaths to clear her head, and took the arm he offered her to walk up the steps.

Mark rang the doorbell, then smiled at her as they waited. "I'll have to admit," he said, turning back to stare straight ahead, "the garter belt was a nice surprise." He rocked back on his heels casually, confident.

Ellie couldn't resist knocking him off balance again. "Then I can't imagine what you would've thought of my tattoo." The look on his face was priceless as the front door swung open and a man who identified himself as Patrick pulled her into his home with a friendly handshake.

It appeared they were among the last of about seventy-five to arrive. Cocktails and finger food circulated the room. Laughter and spirited conversation buzzed around them.

"Ellie?" A familiar female voice spoke behind her, and Ellie turned to see her former boss, Joan Wright, walking toward her.

"Joan," Ellie said, delighted, stepping forward to hug the woman.

"How wonderful to see you!" the older woman said. "What brings you to the Beechams'?"

"I do," Mark said, stepping in to introduce himself.

Joan shot an amused glance at Ellie, then said, "Ah, you

must be the new partner.'' She shook his hand, then frowned slightly. ''Is something wrong with your forehead?''

Ellie's eyes and Mark's hand traveled upward. Lipstick kisses dotted his hairline. She made a frantic wiping motion with her hand, then turned to draw Joan into a conversation about the arts center.

''And the commission is going well?'' Joan's eyes asked more questions than her lips.

Ellie nodded. ''The preliminary work on the painting is done. I hope to get down to business tomorrow.''

''I'll let you ladies talk,'' Mark said, inclining his just-cleaned head. ''Excuse me.'' Ellie felt a curious sense of loss as he walked away. Darn, she was getting much too used to having this man around.

''Hi.''

Ellie turned to see Mark's secretary, Monica, standing next to her and Joan. Ellie made the introductions.

''So,'' Monica said, her tone silky with innuendo, ''how's it going with you and Mark?''

''Oh, we're just friends,'' Ellie assured her.

''Mark is quite a catch,'' she said.

Ellie smiled. ''I'm not fishing,'' she said, then steered the conversation in a safer direction. ''Joan, I thought you and Manny were going someplace tonight.''

Joan's eyes twinkled mischievously, then she moved her head slightly to indicate someone across the room.

Ellie turned to look and nearly swallowed her tongue. Manny, looking feminine and elegant in a brunette wig and long navy dress, stood chatting with none other than Ray Ivan, senior partner. He glanced up and caught her eye, then gave her a tiny shrug of bewilderment. She beckoned him frantically, but even as Manny tried to break away, Ivan followed him with a hand at his elbow. A finger of fear nudged Ellie's stomach.

While Ray and Joan exchanged greetings, Ellie pulled Manny down and whispered furiously, ''What are you doing here dressed like that?''

He grinned. ''I look fabulous, don't I?''

"Manny!"

He pouted prettily. "Relax, would you? It's a joke—Joan thought it would be hilarious to crash a stuffy gig. I had no idea it was the same party you were going to." He grinned and lowered his voice. "I love fooling the straight ones, and I think this Ivan guy is loaded."

"He's Mark's partner, you idiot!"

Manny looked hurt. "But he likes me."

"He likes *Molly,*" she said, using his stage name. "There's a big difference."

"Joan and I are splitting in a few minutes, anyway."

"Don't do anything foolish—Ray just caught us practically naked in the car. Mark is worried to death."

Joan and Monica slipped away. Ray Ivan stepped to Manny's side and smiled at Ellie. "Are you a friend of Molly's?"

"Ellie's my roommate," Manny purred in a low, silky voice. "She's here with Mark Blackwell."

Ellie smiled tightly. *Gee, thanks, friend.*

"Blackwell?" Ivan's eyebrows shot up. "I gather you are, er, close."

Embarrassment flooded over her and she floundered for something to say.

"They're practically married," Manny assured him, patting his arm.

MARK WANDERED OVER to a drink tray and picked up a martini, then scanned the room for Ivan. He needed to extend an apology for what had happened, and he wanted to get it over with. Not sure what he'd say when he did find him, Mark just prayed the right words would come to him. He removed the lipstick-stained handkerchief from his pocket. Between cat allergies and various mishaps, he'd have to remember to carry two hankies with him when Ellie was around. He used the soiled cloth to wipe the sweat from his forehead.

Raising his glass to take another sip, he glanced back to Ellie and choked on the liquid in his throat. Ray Ivan stood talking to her and an attractive brunette. He hurried over to the group as unobtrusively as possible.

"Blackwell!" Ivan boomed. "Glad to see you finally came—I mean, made it—er, good to see you, son." Mark felt the heat climb up his neck as he shook the senior partner's hand.

"Good to see you, sir."

Ivan gestured to the striking woman at his side. "I assume you've met Molly since she's your lovely fiancée's roommate."

So, she had another roommate. "No, I haven't had the pleasure—" His hand stopped in midair. "Did you say fiancée, sir?"

Mark and Ellie exchanged panicked glances, then spoke at the same time.

"I'm not really—"

"She's not really—"

Ivan raised his eyebrows. "What's that, Mark?"

Mark thought about the picture they'd presented earlier to his conservative partner who'd been married for forty years. Mark reached over to put an arm around Ellie's shoulders and squeezed her against him. "Yes, she is lovely, isn't she? Could I have a word with you in private, sir?"

"Certainly."

Mark loosened his grip on Ellie and steered the senior partner to a quiet doorway. "Sir, I want to apologize for what you saw—"

Ivan raised his hand and waved Mark's words away. "Perfectly natural for a man and his bride-to-be, son. When's the big day?"

Mark's mind raced. "Well, we really haven't discussed a day, sir."

"Molly told me you and Miss Sutherland met when she came to the office to paint your portrait a few days ago. Love at first sight, eh?" The older man chuckled. "You're a lucky man, Mark, with good taste. I like to see my partners settle down, become family men. It's important to the firm's image, you know." He winked at Mark, then turned to the room at large and stepped forward. "Everyone," he called, "may I have your attention?"

Dread ballooned in the pit of Mark's stomach as the room quieted.

"I'd like to propose a toast. To our new partner, Mr. Mark Blackwell, who has two reasons to celebrate tonight."

Mark's bowels twisted.

"Raise your glasses with me to honor him and his bride-to-be, Ms. Ellie Sutherland."

The room erupted into gasps and applause. Mark swayed, but caught himself on the door frame, then swung his gaze to Ellie. He pleaded for forgiveness with his eyes. A bewildered smile froze on her face as she nodded to those around her.

Mark soon found himself engulfed by well-wishers. Patrick seemed especially surprised and elbowed him. "You sly dog, what was all that nonsense the other day about remaining single?"

"What can I say?" Mark said, conjuring up a tight smile, his stomach cramping.

"Dinner's served," Patrick's wife announced.

Ellie watched Ray Ivan walk Manny to the door, and to her horror, plant a kiss on her roomie's smooth cheek. Manny waved to her gaily, and she raised her hand halfheartedly in response. Her mind still reeled when Mark took her arm. As they walked toward their table, she whispered, "An engagement wasn't part of the deal. What's going on?"

"I'll explain later," he muttered. "Just remember, I've got your cat."

Ellie reached for another rum and cola as they passed a drink tray and finished it before they were seated. He held out a chair for her at one of the six-person, cloth-covered tables and took the adjacent seat on the end. His leg nudging hers when he spread his napkin across his knee sent tremors through her body.

She knew the alcohol had affected her, but the events of the evening were taking their toll, as well. First, his assault on her senses in the car, then Manny showing up, and now everyone thought they were engaged. She nearly laughed out loud at the irony. She wondered what he would do if she stood on the table and announced that he'd hired her to make his mother hate her, and that a pregnant cat was the only reason she'd come with him tonight?

Well, not the only reason, she conceded, choosing a skewered scallop from a platter on the table. She studied his face as he talked to the man on his right. Mark was one great-looking man, and right now the pheromones were running in her favor. So what if his interest in her was short-lived? There were worse things than having a raging three-week affair with a gorgeous wealthy man.

Time to have some fun.

She slipped off her shoe and snaked her foot around his ankle. Mark jerked his head toward her a fraction, and seemed to stumble on his words, but continued speaking to his companion. Ellie smiled seductively, then worried his shin and calf with her traveling toes. Mark shot her a sharp glance, obviously trying to concentrate on his conversation. Popping the scallop into her mouth, she rolled it on her tongue suggestively. Mark swallowed visibly and shook his head as if in warning, then turned back to the man.

Smothering a giggle, she extended her left leg farther over her right and nudged his knee open. She ran her foot down the inside of his thigh. Suddenly, he jerked again, his hand grabbing her foot to halt its progress. She tried to pull away, but he held her steadfast, and suddenly his other hand claimed her foot, as well. His face was averted from her and he remained deep in conversation.

Teasingly, he swept his finger across the pad of her stockinged foot, sending shudders up Ellie's spine. Her toes crinkled in response, but he slowly and sensuously inserted a large finger between her big toe and its neighbor. Rhythmically, he explored the shallow valley, running the length of his finger in, then out, in, then out.

The ability, as well as the desire, to withdraw her plundered foot vanished. Ellie relaxed into her chair as much as possible without drawing attention to herself, then began squeezing her toes together, clasping his finger harder and harder. As the minutes passed, she grew moist between her thighs, imagining his strong fingers dipping elsewhere. As his finger became more forceful, she increased the pressure. Faster and faster he plunged. Ellie could feel her body pulse inside in tune with his finger's song. The tension mounted, mounted...

"OOOOooooooHHHHhhhhhhh!" she screamed, bringing her hand down upon the table with a solid smack. Every eye in the room turned to her, and even Mark seemed surprised, his ministrations halting momentarily.

"Are you all right, dear?" the woman next to her asked, leaning closer.

Ellie recovered, sitting ramrod straight. "Oh!" she repeated, slapping the table again, "Oh, boy, are these scallops good!" She popped several into her mouth to illustrate, smiling and nodding to everyone at her table, then waving assurance to Patrick's wife across the room. Every woman at the table lunged for a portion.

Afraid to look at Mark, Ellie kept her eyes turned away. What would he think of her now? She withdrew her ravaged foot from his relaxed hands and stretched her cramped toes. Who could have guessed learning to pick up pencils with her toes would come in handy one day?

When at last she chanced a glance at him, his eyes were still on her, slightly widened with an expression that asked, "Was that what I think it was?" She chewed on her bottom lip and nodded ever so slightly.

At her affirmation, amazement washed over Mark. He, too, had become aroused during their little game under the table, but he couldn't believe she'd really—

"As I was saying." The man to his right laid a hand on Mark's arm to resume their conversation. Mark frowned at him, and in the few seconds he broke eye contact with Ellie, she disappeared from sight. Confused, Mark craned his head to search the room, then noticed the tablecloth moving at her place setting. Then he felt her crawl over his feet. Mark stiffened in disbelief, then noticed other people at the table jump, then frown and shift in their seats. She was obviously traveling the length of the table.

He excused himself once again from the man bending his ear. With a quick glance around, Mark swallowed and, as inconspicuously as possible, bent over, then cautiously pulled up the white tablecloth.

For the second time tonight, he was treated to a mouthwatering view of Ellie's rump, but Mark didn't have time to stop and ponder his good fortune. "Ellie!" he whispered sharply. She had to back up, her rear coming very close to his face, in order to twist around and look over her shoulder.

"What?" she retorted, clearly inconvenienced.

"What the hell are you doing?" he whispered.

"Looking for my shoe," she said simply, slurring her words slightly.

"Get out from under there and I'll find it for you," he said, trying to remain patient.

Suddenly, two other heads joined them under the table, both male. "Is there a problem?" asked one fellow who had been paying rapt attention to Ellie all evening.

"No!" Mark barked.

"I can't find my shoe," Ellie said, pouting.

"Well, now," said the other man, tsk-tsking at Ellie, "that will never do."

Mark sighed in exasperation. "For God's sake, Ellie, get out from under there!"

But now nearly everyone at the table was peering beneath the cloth and asking if something was wrong.

Mark reached forward and grabbed Ellie by her upper arm, then steered her out backward. When she stood up and plopped down in her seat, her hairstyle a little worse for wear, Mark ground his teeth in frustration. Their table companions were slow in rejoining them topside, as if Ellie had found something wonderful under the table and they wanted to experience it, too.

"Is this what you're looking for?" The chatty fellow to his right held up a black pump. Sex appeal fairly dripped off the stiletto heel.

"Oh, thank you," Ellie said, grinning, then she reached across the china and crystal to retrieve it. The man looked curiously pleased, until his wife elbowed him sharply in the ribs.

Mark closed his eyes and counted to ten. When he opened them, Ellie was walking away from the table, presumably to find a bathroom, but wearing both shoes, thank goodness. He watched her hips sway, then suddenly realized nearly every man in the room feasted on the same sight. This woman packed a powerful punch.

Mark felt a ridiculous urge to follow her, lock the bathroom door, lift her onto a porcelain sink and wrap her legs around his waist. If a little foot flirting sent her into orbit, what kind of reaction could he elicit with no holds barred? And where would he find her tattoo? Shoulder? Hip? He swallowed. Bikini line?

A tap on his right shoulder startled him. A smiling waiter set a plate of exquisitely arranged salad in front of him, and he was glad to have his attention diverted for the time being. That woman was going to be the death of him, or at least his career. He would eventually need a wife who could entertain a group on this scale, but not one who could double as the entertainment.

Ellie returned a few minutes later, looking refreshed. She nodded at him when she took her seat, smiling brightly. He noticed the color in her cheeks seemed high, and he assumed it had something to do with the amount of rum she'd ingested since they'd arrived. Not that he blamed her, with everything that had happened. Engaged. How on earth was he going to get out of this mess?

She seemed a little flustered still, making small talk with the ladies at the table, one of them his secretary, Monica. He felt a sharp pang of guilt at the questions she had to answer. Yes, she was so proud of her fiancé for making partner. She patted his hand. No, they hadn't shopped for a ring yet. Yes, they planned to have several children. Mark choked on a cherry tomato, but was saved by the gabby man who pounded him hard between the shoulder blades.

Children? Mark patted his mouth with a linen napkin. Would he make a good father? Would Ellie make a good mother? He studied her profile as she spoke to someone across the table, nodding and smiling. She was a beauty, no doubt.

Her features were elfin, small and chiseled. Her blond hair was cropped in short layers, a style only a woman with exquisite features could wear with panache. With her outgoing nature and easy smile, Mark suddenly knew she would be a wonderful mother—romping with her children, singing and dancing to keep them entertained, finger painting the walls if necessary. He smiled and Ellie turned to him at that instant, coming up short at something she read in his eyes. Mark blinked to clear his head and she visibly relaxed.

For the rest of the meal, Mark tried desperately to concentrate on anything but the woman beside him. He puzzled over the power she seemed to wield on his senses. This attraction—it seemed almost supernatural. Not one single aspect of Ellie Sutherland set her apart from any number of beautiful women he'd met, but in totality, she was sensational. Ellie defied science because her whole far outweighed the sum of her parts. The woman was walking synergy.

And he was completely taken by her.

Mark's hands shook slightly as alarms went off in his ears. He'd read about this in men's magazines—and it didn't bode well for his future as a bachelor. No sir, he wasn't about to don the albatross of commitment when he'd just reached a zenith in his career. Yet even as he nodded his head resolutely, Mark's chest clogged with dread when he thought about taking Ellie home and being alone with her. The answer? Stall as long as possible, of course.

"HOW MUCH LONGER?" Ellie whispered a few hours later, trying to smile. Only a few guests lingered over coffee. She could feel her eyelids dragging, threatening to close for good. She'd had no chance to talk to Mark about their abrupt engagement, and she wanted to be somewhat awake on the ride home.

Mark squinted at his watch. "You're right," he said. "We should be going."

They said their goodbyes to their hosts, and a few minutes later they were off.

She waited until they had driven a couple of miles in silence before she cleared her throat. "Well?" she asked.

Mark glanced sideways. "Well what?"

Ellie sighed. "Well, what the heck is going on?"

He passed a hand over his face and pinched the bridge of his nose, squinting. "Believe me, I was as surprised as you were at Ivan's announcement. He's old-fashioned and, after witnessing our little, er, display, he must have arrived at his own conclusion."

Manny's offhand comment to Ivan about she and Mark being "practically married" crossed Ellie's mind, but she didn't mention it. She angled her body toward him. "Why didn't you correct him?"

In the dim interior, she saw his shoulders fall in defeat. "He started telling me how important it was to him that all his partners be settled down, you know—family men—and I couldn't tell him the truth. Next thing I knew, he was toasting our engagement."

Ellie's heart drooped. Mark Blackwell's career meant more to him than anything else in the world. Maybe she'd caught his eye, or rather, his crotch, for a few days because of these pheromones, but she was fooling herself if she thought she'd ever be able to compete with his first love—his job. He had no room for a woman in his life, least of all a woman like her.

"I'm sorry you got dragged into this," he said, reaching over to grasp her hand. "It'll die down in a few weeks, and I'll simply say we broke it off." He squeezed her fingers. "By the way, Ivan seemed taken with your roommate Molly. Why haven't you mentioned her before?"

His hand was so warm, his touch so welcome. Ellie said nothing and just stared at his fingers. "It never came up," she mumbled distractedly. Just a few hours ago she'd told herself to seize the moment. And that was before she knew he could induce her to orgasm, fully dressed and in a crowded room. She felt heat travel up her face. Would he kiss her good-night, or had she scared him off completely? Surely he'd guessed how long she'd been celibate if toe sex sent her over the edge.

When he parked in front of her building, he hesitated slightly. "It's okay," Ellie rushed to assure him. "You don't have to walk me up." She scrambled to loosen her seat belt and find her purse.

"No," he said, turning off the ignition. "I want to."

They walked quickly and quietly into her building and up the stairs. Ellie's heart pounded furiously as she fumbled with the key. Mark took it from her, then unlocked the door easily. The door swung inward, creaking, and darkness stretched before them. Was it her imagination, or had her bed suddenly become a living, breathing entity, palpitating and calling to them from down the hall and behind a closed door?

"Coffee?" she squeaked, flipping on the kitchen light.

"Sure," Mark answered. "A shot of caffeine for the drive home won't hurt." He smiled at her, lowering himself into a kitchen chair. She rummaged nervously for a filter, and managed to get the coffeemaker going within a few tense minutes. "Well," she said brightly, turning to face Mark. "What an interesting evening." She bent to remove her shoes, nudging them under a chair as she rubbed one throbbing arch.

"Yes," Mark agreed in a choked voice. She glanced up to see his eyes riveted on her stockinged feet, and she immediately realized her mistake. She watched as Mark moved in slow motion, standing and reaching for her, pulling her into his arms. Lifting her face to his, she offered her lips to him. His mouth descended on hers, his lips moving hungrily, as if he were a starved man and she a bountiful fare.

Ellie's knees weakened and she swayed into him, twining her arms around his neck for support. He groaned and his voice vibrated inside her mouth, inciting her to respond in kind. Drawing her against him, he lifted her off the ground to settle fully against his arousal. Wild barbs of desire knifed through her as Ellie inhaled the scent of his skin, felt his need for her pushing against her stomach. Mark's hands slid over her back and waist, gripping, massaging, caressing. She felt her nipples bud and bloom against his chest, and raised one leg to hook around his thigh. Immediately, his hands sought her lace-covered rear, exposed by her movement. His breathing became more ragged, until he finally raised his head.

"Ellie," he whispered hoarsely. "I'd like to see that tattoo."

She smiled languidly, desire and…love?…expanding her heart. She might regret this tomorrow, but tomorrow lay a world away, and tonight she needed to live. "I can't walk unless you put me down," she said, referring to her dangling toes.

In response, he swung her up into his arms. "Where's your bedroom?" he asked, his eyes dark with passion. Ellie directed him, her arms still around his neck, her pulse beating out of control during their brief journey. Mark lay her on the bed, then left her long enough to close the door. The only light came from a small window. She watched him move across the room, his movements unhurried. When he returned, he was removing his tie.

"Let me," she said, reaching for him. She sat up, and with deft fingers, made short work of his shirt buttons, then stripped the garment from his back. How many times had she thought of him standing before her like this, bare-chested, the way he looked in his office when she'd taken his picture? He was breathtaking. His hands stilled her when she moved to his waistband.

"I want to see you," he breathed. "I have to see you." Blazing a trail across her skin, his hands enveloped her, moving around to find the zipper at her back. Ellie heard the slide of the enclosure giving way, and felt the fabric fall from her shoulders. Mark leaned toward her, easing her onto the soft comforter, and slipped the dress to her waist. Instantly he found her lace-covered breasts, kissing and suckling through the fabric. Ellie moaned and arched her back, thrusting the small peaks up for his onslaught. Without taking his mouth from her, he lifted her hips and eased the dress down her legs. She heard the whoosh of the fabric as it landed somewhere on the floor.

When Mark drew back long enough to take in the sight of Ellie lying before him in black bra, panties, garter belt and stockings, he had to clench his teeth in resolve. *Hold on, man, hold on.* The fact that his body had been in a near-perpetual state of arousal throughout the evening convinced him his present control bordered on tenuous, at best. Slender and smooth, she was beautifully arched to reveal endless valleys and peaks to explore. From her shapely collarbone to the divot in her flat stomach, to the valley between her thighs hidden by her raised knees. Where to begin? Hours seemed woefully inadequate to sample Ellie's gifts, yet his body told him he had scant minutes left.

A loud groan escaped him as he stretched out beside her, capturing her mouth in a kiss that threatened to be his undoing when she wriggled against him. She turned in his arms and he managed to undo her bra, sending her small, full breasts tumbling into his hands. He dipped his head to taste their richness and grew heady from the overwhelming desire flooding his body. The intoxicating scent of her skin took him near the brink. Such exquisite torture he'd never had to endure before, and Mark knew he couldn't take much more.

Her small fingers splayed across his back then down to his waist, struggling briefly with his zipper, then helping him drag the pants down with her feet. He kicked them off, his breath leaving him when Ellie reached to clasp his stiff manhood. She stroked him within milliseconds of exploding. He grabbed her hand to still her movements.

"I'm not superhuman," he groaned, rolling over to lie between her legs. Mark took a few deep breaths to steady himself, then undid her garter belt. Thoughts of slowly rolling her thigh-high stockings down and off her pretty feet flickered through his mind, but he knew he'd be lucky to remove her panties in one piece. Hot need billowed in him, and he tugged her underwear down hurriedly, raising her knees to speed the process. A glimpse of dense dark blond curls registered in his mind before he returned to the cradle between her legs. His heat-seeking member rushed to her entrance.

"Mark," she whispered, "I'm not protected."

Sanity flashed and he lowered his head. "Of course," he said, then gritted his teeth. Sighing, he gently rolled off her and lay still, fighting to gain control. "I'm sorry," he said. "I lost my head."

Ellie sat up and reached to open a drawer in her nightstand. "I have regular and extra-large," she announced, rummaging through its contents.

Mark bounced upright. "Whichever you think."

She peered at him, a smile playing on her lips. "Extra-large."

It seemed to take hours for her to roll the condom into place, and Mark shook with his need to make love to her. At last, she lay back and pulled him to her, her neck arched, leaving it exposed for his kisses. He licked at the hollow beneath her chin, then found an earlobe to nuzzle as he eased himself into her warmth. Their moans mingled as he stilled, taking a few seconds to experience her. She tightened around him and Mark tensed to hold on a little longer. Just long enough for her to—

A long scream escaped her lips and she clawed his back in the throes of her passion. Amazement registered for an instant, but quickly gave way to gratitude as he began to move within her, feeling free now to expend himself. The mewling sounds she moaned into his ear urged him on. He felt his senses soar, his body tense in preparation for release, then shuddered again and again as ecstasy delivered him from his suffering.

Not until minutes later, as he lay nuzzling a pert nipple and feeling her heart beat against his cheek, did Mark realize he still hadn't noticed a tattoo.

MARK OPENED HIS EYES, disoriented at first. Then he remembered he slept in Ellie's bed. He turned his head to see the clock. Three in the morning.

Usually he lingered with a lover until morning, but now he had an overwhelming need to go home. Or more to the point, to get out of Ellie's bed. The walls of her bedroom, covered with eclectic groupings of prints and various bric-a-brac, suddenly seemed to close in on him. As noiselessly as possible, he got up, gathered his clothing and dressed. He winced at the sight of the wadded pile he'd made of the dress in which she'd bewitched him and every man at the party. Carefully, he picked it up and folded it neatly, placing it on the dressing table.

Mark walked back to the bed, planning to kiss her, but instead stopped to watch her sleep, her breasts easing up and down with her deep, even breathing. A tingling sensation settled in his chest and made his own breathing difficult. After a last glance, he opened her bedroom door, stepped into the hall and closed it behind him.

Silently, he retraced his steps to the front door, then stopped when he realized someone was unlocking the door from the hallway. His heart raced. A burglar? Then Mark relaxed. It was probably just one of Ellie's roommates.

Molly stepped inside, then her eyes widened in fear, a key dangling from a manicured hand raised to defend herself.

Mark rushed to explain in a loud whisper, "I'm Mark Blackwell, Ellie's, uh, friend. We met earlier this evening." He smiled apologetically and pointed to the door. "I was just leaving." He stepped into the hall and closed the door behind him.

The short drive north seemed interminable, not just because Mark fought falling asleep, but because his big lonely bed no longer seemed so inviting. Ellie's sleep-softened face came to him, and her plump nipples sitting atop her breasts like puffs of pink whipped cream. He moistened his lips involuntarily, and nearly ran off the shoulder of the highway. Loud music from his stereo and a full-blast air conditioner got him home safely.

The clock on his nightstand read ten minutes past four. Mark began to strip off his clothes again, then grimaced as his shirt raked across his uncomfortably tender back. One glance in the mirror showed why, and his mouth fell open. Bright red welts and a few tiny drops of dried blood marked his back where Ellie had clawed him in her passion. Too tired to register more than passing astonishment, Mark climbed into bed. He had just closed his eyes, when his nose began to itch. He rubbed a knuckle over it, annoyed. At the same time, something warm and furry touched his foot. Mark shouted and sat up in the bed, scrambling for the light.

A muffled yowl sounded under the covers. Mark jumpe out of the bed and watched the lump travel beneath the cover to the pillow where his head had rested. Esmerelda poked he orange head out to peer at him angrily.

"Scat," Mark barked, buck-naked and waving his arms The cat blinked. A fit of sneezing seized him, sending him i search of a handkerchief. "Get out of my bed," he com manded, gesturing again. Esmerelda yawned. When Mar reached for her, she flattened her ears against her head, an flung an evil hiss toward him. He jumped back, wondering i the beast had been declawed. Deciding he'd rather not find ou tonight, Mark tramped noisily down the hall to a guest room sneezing the entire way.

As he punched down a lumpy pillow, Mark cursed sourly He'd left one unsettling she-cat only to come home to another

7

Ellie awoke with the most delicious feeling in her bones. Her hazy mind struggled to remember what event had triggered this languid, buoyant state. She'd won the lottery…no. Her paintings were being offered at an exclusive auction…no. She'd slept with Mark Blackwell…

Ellie's eyes popped open. Yes! A tentative lifting of her knee triggered soreness in several little-used muscles, and she grimaced. Sitting up and pulling the sheet around her breasts, she scanned the room for evidence of Mark's presence. Her dress had been folded neatly. The indention in the pillow next to hers felt cold.

A foreign scent assailed her nostrils. Sex. Their fragrances lingered on the morning air. Ellie pulled her pillow higher against the headboard, and reclined against it with a sigh. On impulse, she pulled the other pillow over her face and inhaled his aroma, then settled it across her stomach. Her heart raced. Now what?

A knock at her door stymied her rising panic. "Ellie, are you up?" Manny's voice was soft but insistent.

"Just a minute," she called, reaching to pull a short terry robe from its home on the bedpost. She still wore her stockings and loosened garter belt, although the garments had twisted uncomfortably. She tied the frayed robe belt around her waist and tucked the ends under her hips, then straightened the covers around her. "You can come in."

"Breakfast in bed," Manny announced grandly, entering with a laden bed tray.

Ellie grinned. "And what, may I ask, is the occasion?"

Manny smiled wide, his eyes knowing, as he set the tray

on her lap. "Your introduction back into a morally bankrupt society."

"What makes you think—"

"Don't bother denying it." Manny held up his hand. "I passed Mark on his way out this morning." He smiled, triumphant. "So?" he prompted, settling in cross-legged at the foot of the bed.

"So what?" she said, taking a bite of toast.

"For heaven's sake, give me the details."

As Ellie chewed, the events of the entire evening began to resurface in florid detail. She winced.

"Come on, 'fess up," Manny urged. "You set Ray Ivan straight about your engagement, right?"

Ellie bit into her bottom lip.

Manny's eyes rolled back. "You didn't?"

"There didn't seem to be a good time to mention it."

"Unbelievable," he said, shaking his head. "Your life is better than a soap opera. So tell me, how did you go from being a fake fiancée—" he leaned over to retrieve a stray earring from the floor "—to a genuine seductress?" He dangled the bauble for emphasis.

The quick sip of juice did not lessen the heat that rushed to Ellie's face. "He brought me home, then I asked him in for coffee, and the next thing I knew, he was carrying me in here." She shrugged.

"Well, that explains the full pot of cold coffee," Manny said sarcastically, then he brightened. "Was it earth-shattering?"

Ellie tried to hold back a grin, but couldn't. "I can't remember having two really great orgasms in one night."

"Two? I'm impressed. Didn't think Mr. Republican had it in him."

"Well, one occurred at the dinner party—"

"What?"

"It's not what you think. We were fully clothed, and sitting down. After you left, I got a little tipsy and started playing footsie with his...well, anyway, he grabbed my foot and the next thing I know, I'm screaming like a banshee in the middle of the appetizer course."

"You got off on him playing with your *feet?* You were in worse shape than I thought, woman." He howled with laughter, pounding his knees with his fists. Wiping his eyes, he suddenly sobered. "Has anything like that ever happened before? I mean, do you think the pheromones had something to do with your reaction?"

Ellie took another drink. "No, it's never happened before, and yes, I think it has everything to do with the pills." She hadn't meant to sound so glum.

"Did Ray Ivan ask about me?"

"Manny, you're playing with fire."

"I think it's fun."

"He's a sweet, *straight* old widower. If you took off your skirt, he'd probably have heart failure."

He waved off her concern. "It doesn't matter, El, I'll never see the man again. By the way—" he wagged his eyebrows "—when will you see Mark?"

Ellie gasped and looked at the clock. "I have to be at his office for a sitting in forty-five minutes! What am I going to say to him after last night?"

"Hmm." Manny tapped his cheek in mock deep thought. "How about 'thank you'?"

"THANK YOU," Ellie said as Mark held the door to the office building open wide enough to allow her to wheel in her bike. They'd arrived at the same time, Mark rounding the corner from the parking garage just in time to see Ellie ride up in front of the building.

He smiled stiffly at her, feeling awkward. She certainly looked chipper today in pink bike shorts and a glove-fitting zebra-print tank top. But then, she didn't have to apply salve to her battle wounds, then don a starched dress shirt for a sitting. Her dangling black claw earrings were a staunch reminder of the injuries she'd inflicted last night. Still, he had to admit it was the greatest sex he'd experienced. He rolled his shoulders, trying to ease his taut skin as they walked through the reception area to the elevators. Neither of them spoke on the ride up. She looked completely at ease, and he didn't have a clue what to say about last night. Finally, she broke the silence.

"How's Esmerelda?" she asked, reaching over to extract a long orange hair from his shirtsleeve.

Mark frowned and brushed his sleeve with his hand, dislodging more hairs. He promptly sneezed. "Your cat has taken up residence in my bedroom. In my bed, to be more precise."

"Really? She hardly ever leaves her bed at night. She must be under a lot of stress, being in new surroundings. Or there could be something wrong with the room where you put her bed."

A flash of annoyance surfaced, but he forced patience into his voice. "Your feline already has the run of my house. What could possibly be wrong?" The bell sounded and the doors slid open.

Ellie stepped off the elevator and guided her bicycle toward his office. "The room where you put her bed, what color is it?"

"Blue."

Ellie smacked her handlebars with one hand and nodded. "That's it—she hates blue."

Mark took a mighty breath and rubbed one temple. His aggravated allergies were giving him a headache. And now the allergen didn't approve of his decor.

"Hey, you two," Patrick called, walking toward them, smiling.

"Oh, damn," Mark muttered, then donned an appropriate smile. "Hey, yourself," he said as Patrick drew nearer. "Nice party."

"You two were the spotlight," Patrick insisted, then turned to Ellie. "And I can't tell you what a pleasure it is to meet the woman who's tamed this maverick. I never thought I'd see the day Mark Blackwell settled down."

Ellie shrugged and nodded, her expression one of agreeable shock. "Amazing, isn't it?"

"Actually, Patrick—" Mark began.

"Good morning, all!" Ray Ivan boomed from down the hall. "Well, if it isn't the happy couple." He walked up and patted Ellie's arm, then clapped Mark on his raw back, sending spasms of pain down his spine.

Mark inhaled sharply. "Good morning, sir."

Ivan pointed to the canvas and paint-stained tackle box strapped to the panniers of Ellie's bike. "Working on the portrait, today, are we?"

She smiled wide, her eyes bright. "We sure are."

Mark's partner nodded agreeably, then said. "Listen, kids, let me know as soon as you set a wedding date, because it's been my policy to start a brokerage account for my married employees as a college fund for their children. Right, Patrick?"

"Right," Beecham said.

"Children?" Mark and Ellie said in unison.

"Monica told me last night that you plan to have a big family," Ivan said.

Mark remembered Ellie's words at the dinner table and felt his underarms grow moist. They'd very nearly started a family last night. He looked at Ellie, and she looked back, eyes wide.

Ivan laughed, slapping Mark's back again, twice. "Didn't mean to put you on the spot. Just let me know, Blackwell. And congratulations again, you picked a beauty." He winked at Ellie, then engaged Patrick in a conversation as they walked away.

"I need some aspirin," Mark said, moving toward his office.

Once the door closed behind them, Ellie took a deep breath. Trying to sound casual as she lowered her kickstand, she said, "Why did you leave in the middle of the night?"

"Huh?" Mark swallowed the pills he'd shaken into his palm. "Oh, well, I knew I had to come in here this morning, and there were some papers at home I wanted to go over." His voice sounded vague. "And don't forget about the cat," he added, his eyes darting around the room. "I had to check on her."

Ellie frowned slightly. He wasn't very convincing. Obviously he preferred hurrying home to handle work details to dawdling in her bed. A career man, through and through.

"By the way," he said, "I ran into Molly while I was leaving your apartment. I didn't see a third bedroom. Where does she stay?"

Ellie's mind raced. "Uh, she stays in Manny's room."

"Ivan will be heartbroken," he said.

"Oh, they have an open relationship," she improvised. "You never see them together." She swallowed, then scrambled to change the subject. "This session shouldn't take too long. All I really need to do is a composition sketch."

"Sure," he said in a distracted tone. "Where do you want me?"

They locked gazes. Ellie's heart pounded as snatches of their lovemaking spun through her mind.

Mark cleared his throat. "We really should talk—"

The phone rang, breaking the spell.

"I'll get set up," she explained, gesturing to her supplies. She kicked herself mentally. Mark Blackwell was the epitome of her father in his younger days. Hadn't she always promised herself she deserved more than her mother had put up with? So why on earth was she entertaining thoughts of a future with him? It had to be the pheromones.

She heard Mark push a button. "Mark Blackwell," he said, all business.

"Marcus!" his mother's voice screeched over the speakerphone.

Ellie watched as Mark rounded his desk to sit down, worry in his face. "Mom? Where are you calling from? Is everything all right?"

"No!" she continued more shrilly than before. "How can everything be all right when I arrive at Stella's house for bridge and she announces to me that my own son is getting married?"

"Mom—"

"And *please* don't tell me it's to that fruitcake you brought to the reunion. I lived in the bathroom for three days—"

Mark stabbed the intercom button and picked up the receiver, then spun around in the chair, his back to Ellie, murmuring low into the phone.

Oh, great, Ellie thought, the woman *does* hate me. And the only thing she needed in her life less than a workaholic boyfriend was a workaholic mama's boy.

"Mom, don't worry," she heard him say. "It's all a big mistake that got way out of hand." He paused. "Mom, if I were getting married, don't you think you'd be the first to know?"

Probably even before the bride, Ellie mused as she unpacked her supplies.

"Yeah, you can reassure Stella she doesn't have to buy an expensive wedding gift, after all. I have to go, Mom. I'll call you later." He hung up and sighed. "Sorry about that." He stood and walked toward her, shrugging sheepishly. "Mom is a little excitable, if you hadn't noticed."

"Oh, really?" Ellie said, injecting a hint of sarcasm into her voice. "Did you set her straight about our little pretend engagement?"

He did have the good grace to blush. "I told her it was all a mistake."

"She didn't sound like the same woman who's desperate for you to get married."

He smiled wryly, shrugging again. "I guess when it comes right down to it, she doesn't want another woman in my life."

"More to the point, she doesn't want *me* in your life."

Mark pursed his lips. "That's my fault. I shouldn't have asked you to pull all those stunts at the reunion. I guess my behavior was childish." He looked into her eyes, and reached over to touch her hand. "I'm sorry, Ellie."

His voice and expression were genuine. Ellie blinked furiously to stem her welling tears. "All those stunts" were natural events.

"Where were we?" he asked. Restlessly, he shoved a hand through his light brown hair, leaving it disheveled. For a few seconds, she felt sorry for him. His life had been turned upside down inside a week of meeting her. But then, so had hers.

"You messed it up," she said, reaching up to smooth the

errant strands. His hair felt silky and thick, fresh from a recent shower, she guessed. Memories of twining her hands through it last night came to her, but she brushed them aside. He stood perfectly still, his eyes locked with hers while she fussed with his hair. Desire lurked in the depths of his forest green eyes. And what else? Affection? What might her traitorous eyes be revealing to him? "There," she said, giving his hair a final pat and easing the moment.

"I think we should talk about last night," he said.

"Well, I am curious about the blood on the sheet."

Mark gestured loosely over his shoulder. "I didn't realize your nails were so long." He smiled and added, "Or so effective."

Embarrassment sent heat rushing to her face. Ellie gasped, covering her mouth. "I did that?"

He nodded. "You were the only other person in the bed."

"I'm so sorry, are you okay?"

Now he laughed. "I only regret I won't be in senior gym class tomorrow to gloat in the locker room." He reached for her, and she went to him, her kiss a peace offering.

The phone rang again. They parted. Mark glanced at the display, and reached for the handset. "It's Ray," he said. "Hello, sir." He paused. "Yes, she's still here."

Ellie's eyebrows shot up.

Mark listened for a few seconds, then surprise registered on his face. "Hold on and I'll ask." Mark pushed a button to mute the sound and said, "He wants to take Molly to dinner. Can you arrange it?"

Ellie's stomach dipped. "But Manny—"

"I thought you said they had an open relationship."

"I, uh…Molly's not exactly your partner's type, Mark."

"Okay, she's younger than Ray by a couple of decades, but you have to admit she's showing a little wear herself. He's a young and wealthy sixty-two. She could do worse."

She floundered. "But she hardly knows him…I don't think she'd be comfortable."

"So we'll double."

Her heart pounded. "As in a double date?"

"Sure. It would give me a chance to get to know Ray more informally. And maybe we can find a way to explain away our pseudo-engagement."

"I'm not sure—"

"Help me out, Ellie. I need to redeem myself for that little car-necking incident, which was really your fault, by the way."

"*My* fault?"

He leaned toward her and nuzzled her earlobe. "It wouldn't have happened if you weren't so damned irresistible."

Ellie's pulse jumped erratically. He was right—the episode before the party *had* been her fault. All roads led back to the pheromone pills. "Well..."

He pushed a button to retrieve his partner. "How about the four of us going to dinner? The Lexington Diner? Tonight?" Mark looked at Ellie for affirmation and she nodded resolutely. "Ellie will talk to Molly and get it all set up. I'll pick up the girls and we'll meet you there around seven."

"Thanks," he said to Ellie after he'd hung up. "Ivan hasn't dated at all since his wife passed away. This is a big step for him."

If he only knew how big. Ellie coughed. "I have to go to Underground this afternoon to stand in for an artist friend," she said apologetically. "I guess I'd better get started here."

"Explain to me again what you'll be doing today," he said distractedly.

The Puritan-white canvas she withdrew begged for paint. She loved the faintly pungent odor of newly dried gesso. "I'll be applying a base coat of thin oil paint to develop a working composition—what objects are placed where in the painting." She gestured to the canvas with a dry paintbrush for emphasis.

"I thought it was just me in the painting," he said, grinning.

That smile of his threatened to be her undoing. "It *is* just you, but the background will also have its place in the painting. And the size of your shoulders, face, etcetera, is very important."

His grin deepened. "How low are you going?"

Ellie rolled her eyes. "Just to your chest, Mark." Not that

she wouldn't enjoy painting a full-length portrait of him, and nude, at that. In art school she'd drawn professional nude models who cut a less impressive figure than Mark Blackwell.

"Anyway, the important thing today is to sort out the colors and placement. Then I can begin the detailed work. By the way, the thinned-down paint I'll use now will dry quickly, but once I start layering in color, I'll be using long-drying oils. At that point, it's going to be difficult to transport the canvas," she smiled, suddenly fidgety. "Especially on a bike."

He looked confused. "So?"

Ellie sighed. She hated doing this, it would seem as if she was trying to get him back to her place. "So, since I don't have a studio to work in, I'll have to set up the easel in my apartment and ask you to come there when I need you to, uh...sit." Her face burned, but the situation couldn't be helped.

"And how often would I get to come and...sit?" he asked, leaning close. His dark green eyes danced merrily.

"Not much at first, but then about every other d-day."

His face fell. "Is that all? I've got a better idea. Why don't you set up at my place? I've got plenty of room, and you could take care of—I mean, check in on your cat." He stopped for a moment, concern on his face. "Is it a problem getting to my house that often? I'd hate for you to have to take a taxi every time."

"No," Ellie said slowly, thoughtfully. "I could ride my bike to the train, take the train to the Dunwoody station, then ride the short distance to your house. It's only a couple of blocks." Ellie's mind spun. It did seem like the perfect solution. And she missed Esmerelda terribly.

Mark nodded. "Good, then it's settled."

"But I'd have to be there during the day," Ellie warned.

"I'll give you a key," he said simply. "No big deal."

Sure, Ellie thought miserably. Obviously he didn't perceive their working together in an intimate setting as a big deal. And why would he? He didn't intend for their "relationship" to go anywhere.

Of course, she had more immediate problems to deal with. Like matchmaking between Mark's partner and her transvestite roommate.

8

"*THIS* I'm not sure about," Manny said, drumming his painted fingernails on the kitchen table.

"Me, neither," Ellie admitted, sorting through the junk mail. "But you owe me one for leading Ray Ivan to believe Mark and I are engaged."

Manny threw his hands in the air. "I was only trying to save your reputation. He jumped to his own conclusion."

"Okay, okay. Go to dinner as Molly and you can help us explain the misunderstanding. Then you can make excuses the next time Ray Ivan calls." She lifted a finger in warning. "But no funny stuff."

Manny reached over to toy with a rose petal that had dropped onto the table's surface from the bouquet of a dozen in the delivered vase. "The man does have class," he said, fingering the card with "Molly" written on it. "I take it you haven't told Mark about the real me?"

Ellie chewed the corner of her lip. "No."

His mouth tightened. "I can't blame you. He'd die if he knew he'd come within a hundred feet of a drag queen."

"Manny, Mark's a big boy raised in a big city—he's not *that* naive. But I didn't want to divulge details about your life to a man who was a stranger little more than a week ago." She stood and tossed a handful of envelopes in the trash can. "And once the painting is finished and I'm out of pills, he'll be a stranger again."

"Why do I feel a Barry Manilow song coming on?"

"Look," Ellie said in exasperation. "I need to know if you can pull this off tonight."

"*Moi?* I've been a woman nearly as long as you have, El.

Of course I can pull this off.'' He brightened at the challenge. ''It'll be fun.''

Warning bells sounded in her ears at his exuberance. Manny loved nothing better than performing—she hoped he didn't outdo himself.

Indeed, when Mark picked them up, a bewigged Manny looked a picture of cool, tall, slender femininity in a short wrap skirt and fitted jacket. Ellie, on the other hand, was sweating profusely in her red silk shift by the time they reached the restaurant. She hadn't expected Mark to recognize Manny—she sometimes had to look closely herself to believe the metamorphosis—but still she was a nervous wreck.

The Lexington Diner enjoyed the reputation of being one of the swankiest eateries in the upscale area of Phipps Plaza. Not only was the menu famous, but the establishment also boasted a celebrated orchestra that played big-band tunes behind a large dance floor. According to Mark, all the attorneys at his firm held memberships.

Ray Ivan sat waiting for the group at a secluded table. Everyone exchanged pleasantries. ''You look stunning, my dear,'' he crooned to Manny, standing to pull out his chair. The older man looked flushed and excited. Ellie noted the half-empty wine bottle on the table with a shiver of premonition.

''Thank you,'' Manny responded, his voice honeyed.

The waiter brought more wine posthaste, and Mark ordered appetizers. Ellie didn't take her eyes off the couple across from her, and concentrated hard to hear every word.

''Molly, what do you do for a living?'' Ray asked.

Manny smiled coquettishly. ''I'm a performer.''

''A singer?'' He seemed quite pleased.

''And a dancer,'' Manny confirmed.

Ray leaned in to Manny's ear. Ellie leaned forward to listen. ''I should have known by those legs,'' she heard him say, his words slightly slurred.

''Oh, my!'' Manny jumped, slapping playfully at Ray's hand beneath the table.

''Ellie,'' Mark whispered, ''didn't your mother ever tell you not to eavesdrop? Let's dance and leave them alone for a few minutes.''

''But—''

''Come on.'' He stood and tugged her along behind him.

Thoughts of a masquerading Manny were swept away when Mark pulled her to him in a slow, close waltz. She fused her curves to his hollows, tucking her head beneath his chin, and gave herself up to his liquid movements. He was a wonderful dancer, graceful and strong. She loved the feel of his muscles moving against her, his hips melded to hers, guiding her to the low throb of the music. His hand stroked her lower back, stirring volcanic reactions in her midsection.

''You smell wonderful,'' he breathed into her ear. ''Can I take you home with me?''

Ellie winced. She was oozing pheromones again. *There's nothing quite so romantic as an old-fashioned synthetic chemical reaction.* She lifted her head. ''What about Molly?''

''If things go well, and it looks like they will, I suspect Ray will want to see her home.''

Worry pooled in her stomach. ''I didn't expect Ray to be so…taken with her so quickly.''

''Why not? He's lonely, and she's a striking woman. Let's just let nature take its course.''

Right now at that table, nature is being stood on its ear. Ellie bit her tongue hard.

''So you'll sleep in my bed tonight?'' he murmured.

Ellie lowered her chin to hide her eyes. She was falling for this man, and setting herself up for a fantastic tailspin. ''Let's just let nature take its course,'' she said, settling into his broad chest.

When she opened her eyes a few seconds later, she saw that Manny and Ray had joined the dancers on the floor. Manny held himself rigidly, but Ray's hands were roaming freely. When he grabbed a handful of Manny's rear end, Ellie missed a beat and stepped on Mark's foot.

''Ow,'' he said, chuckling.

''Sorry. We'd better get back to our table—I'm starved.''

She tugged him back to their chairs, and, thankfully, Manny and Ray followed suit.

The waiter came around to take their entrée orders and delivered yet another bottle of wine on the house. Ellie lost count of the glasses Mark's partner downed. When the saucers of escargot arrived, everyone dug in but Ray, who appeared to be well on his way to becoming smashed.

Mark leaned over to whisper to Ellie. "I've never seen Ivan drink like this—he must be nervous."

Ellie nodded, glanced at Manny and swallowed a snail whole. His left eyelash was coming unglued and flapped precariously when he blinked. She looked over at Mark. He, too, had noticed and was studying Manny closely.

"Um, Molly," Ellie said, trying to keep alarm out of her voice.

Manny looked up and Ellie winked hard at him several times, then wagged her eyebrows.

"Is something wrong, Ellie?" Ray asked, exaggerated concern evident in his blurry eyes.

"I, uh..." Ellie's mind raced. "I need to go to the bathroom, and I need Molly to come with me." She jumped up, grabbed Manny by the forearm and dragged him away from the table.

"What is it now?" Manny demanded.

"You're losing an eyelash," she hissed, herding him toward the lounge.

He reached up to finish yanking it off. "Damn, you can't find good adhesive anymore. I've got more in my purse—it'll just take a minute."

They shuffled into the bathroom where Ellie wet a towel to hold to her perspiring face.

Manny leaned into the mirror, carefully reapplying the lash. "Gee, El, Mark's partner is as horny as the brass section of the Atlanta Symphony."

She threw him a sarcastic look. "And you're complaining?"

"Let's just say what little appeal the man *had* evaporated

a vineyard ago. And I don't know how I'm going to get rid of him."

"Maybe our best strategy would be to wait for him to pass out."

"And when do we get to the part about your engagement being a farce?"

"Even if we tell him, he won't remember tomorrow."

"You're right, which is why I'm going to tell him to kiss off."

Ellie's eyes bulged. "You can't! You have to let him down easy so he won't hold it against Mark. You and I got Mark into this mess, we have to see it through."

Manny pointed a long nail at her. "Let's get this straight—I'm doing this for you, not Mark. And believe me, you can't be gentle with men like Ray Ivan. He'll have to be hit over his balding head, or he'll be calling me from now on. This has gone too far. I think we need to tell Mark the truth."

Ellie's throat constricted. "You mean, about you?" Manny's occupation and alter identity would not be within Mark Blackwell's scope of understanding. And she didn't want Manny to be offended by a confrontation.

His face fell. "Are you ashamed of me?"

"Oh, no, Manny," she rushed to assure him. "But Mark is pretty conservative. He might not be very accepting."

"Then let's get Ray away from the table and broaden Mr. Blackwell's horizons."

Ellie felt faint as they left the ladies' room. The only guaranteed outcome of this evening would be a retraction of Mark's invitation to share his bed tonight. Manny stopped at a pay phone outside the lounge and dialed the restaurant's number, asked for Ray Ivan to be paged, then left the handset lying on its side.

"We're back," Manny said brightly as they approached the table.

"Are you okay?" Mark asked Ellie when she claimed her seat. "You look a little pale."

She mumbled she was fine, and took a long drink of wine for courage.

The maître d' appeared. "Mr. Ivan, a phone call for you. Right this way."

Ray straightened his suit, and managed to walk away with only a slight stagger.

The entrées had arrived during their stint in the bathroom. Ellie let a few seconds of silence pass watching Mark eat two bites of rare steak. Her salmon sat untouched.

Manny cleared his throat violently and frowned at her, nodding toward Mark's bent head.

"Mark," Ellie said, moistening her lips. "We have something to tell you."

"What?" he asked, taking a swallow of wine, then proceeding to carve off another cube of prime rib.

She looked at Manny, and he nodded encouragement. Ellie gripped the napkin in her lap into tight fists. "Well, the truth is—"

"The truth is," said Manny in his own voice, "looks can be deceiving."

Mark stared at Manny and blinked, his lips parting slowly. He leaned forward, squinting, then his eyes bulged. "M-Manny?"

Manny lifted a manicured hand in a small wave. "How's it hanging, Mark?"

Mark dropped his silverware with a loud clatter, and felt the blood drain from his face. "Oh...my...God." He gripped the chair arms and gaped at them for interminable seconds. "You're telling me—" His voice was high and shaky. He stopped and looked around, then cleared his throat and began again, this time speaking low and deliberately. "You're telling me I set my partner up with a *man?*"

Ellie winced and Manny nodded.

Mark gripped his head with both hands. "This can't be happening." He looked around hopefully. "Am I on 'Candid Camera'? Please tell me I am." Blood pounded in his ears and he felt faint. He jerked his head around to look at Ellie. "Why the devil didn't you *tell* me?"

"I tried, but you said you needed to make amends for us being naked in the car—"

"*I* wasn't naked—"

"Technically, neither was I—"

"Kids," Manny snarled, "we don't have time for this. Here he comes, and he already asked me to go home with him." Their heads pivoted to see Ray striding toward the table, having eyes only for Manny.

"You have to get out of here," Mark hissed to Manny. "Right now!"

"That won't keep him from calling me and sending flowers," Manny insisted. "I'll have to hurt his feelings sooner or later. We have to nip this in the bud. I've got an idea—work with me."

Ray slid into his seat and flashed them a bleary smile. "False alarm." He moved his chair closer to his date, looping an arm around the back of Manny's chair. "Now, where were we?"

Mark's career flashed before his eyes. Sweat popped out on his forehead, and he downed the glass of wine. Manny leaned forward to whisper something to Ellie, and she nodded in response, her eyes darting to Mark. *What are they up to now?*

"Mr. Ivan," Ellie said sweetly. "Would you like to dance?"

"Well, of course, dear." Ray tore himself away from Manny and accompanied Ellie to the dance floor.

Mark narrowed his eyes at Manny. "Don't even think about asking me to dance."

Manny waved him off, exasperated. "Don't be ridiculous—you're not my type at all. But I do need for you to go to the men's room with me."

"Excuse me?"

"I need to borrow your pants."

"What?"

"Look, for both our sakes, I've got to shake this guy once and for all. Are you with me?"

Cornered and out of options, he gestured toward the rest room and relented stiffly. "This is against my better judgment."

"I'll go first, and you follow in a few minutes."

Manny escaped and Mark played with his empty wineglass for a few seconds, then whistled tunelessly while he watched the second hand on his watch. When exactly one minute had passed, he strolled toward the men's room.

He breathed a sigh of relief to find the room empty. Perhaps Manny had gone home. He'd make excuses to Ray and somehow convince him not to call her, uh, him again.

"Pssst!"

Mark jerked his head toward the sound. One of the stall doors was closed, but no legs or feet were visible.

"Pssst, over here, Mark!"

Mark walked over to the stall and said, "What the hell are you doing?"

"I'm getting undressed."

"Are you suspended in midair?"

"I'm standing on the toilet."

Mark put his hands on his hips. "Did Ellie teach you that trick?"

A man entered the bathroom and walked to the sink, eyeing a large red stain on his lapel. He nodded to Mark and reached for a towel.

"Would you stop clowning around and take off your pants?" Manny whispered loudly.

Mark groaned inwardly. The man's head snapped up. He made wide eye contact with Mark, then turned and bolted out the door.

"Great," Mark said, walking into the adjacent stall. "We just scared a customer to death. He's probably reporting us right now. What are you doing, anyway?"

"I'm going to get Ray off Molly's back. Hurry up—I need your shirt, pants, socks and shoes."

"And what am I supposed to wear in the meantime?"

"Oh, that's right—Ellie says you don't wear undies."

"Does she tell you everything?" Mark sputtered.

"*Every*thing—you can hang on to your jacket for security."

Mark began stripping off his clothes and handed them over the top of the stall. "This had better work."

"Trust me."

"Oh, yeah," Mark said sarcastically. "The man wearing the WonderBra says 'trust me.'"

"Don't knock it till you've tried it."

Why hadn't he worn boxers tonight? Mark felt utterly ridiculous standing naked in his suit jacket and holding his tie in front of his crotch while Manny dressed in his clothes. He wondered briefly if he could be disbarred for public nudity. Probably.

A couple of minutes later, a wad of clothing sailed over the top of the stall. Mark dodged panty hose, girdle, a set of fake boobs, wig, high heels and other mysterious items, watching them settle onto the tiled floor around him. "What's all this crap?" he demanded.

"All that crap is my wardrobe," Manny said hotly. I can't leave it in here—someone might take it. Keep it with you until I get back."

Mark crossed his arms and shook his head in defeat. "I saw this once in a movie. If you leave me stranded with nothing to wear out of here but women's clothes, I'll track you down and kick your butt. You've got ten minutes."

"I'll be back," was Manny's acid response. Mark heard the stall door open and close, then lots of water splashing, then finally Manny exiting the outer door.

A few seconds later, the outer door opened again, this time admitting someone with a slow lazy stride. Mark looked down at his hairy legs and bare feet and imagined how it would look from the other side. He quickly stooped to snatch Manny's clothing from the floor and out of sight. Sweat beaded on his forehead.

"Having problems in there?" the man asked haughtily, walking over to stop in front of the stall.

Mark's heart stopped. He knew that voice.

"Hey, buddy." The man knocked, and raised his voice in a challenge. "I said, are you having problems in there?"

His co-worker, Tony Specklemeyer. The little hotshot who'd come to his office for a showdown over cheating on a client's tax forms. Mark cursed silently, scalding the air. The ambitious little jackass would hang him out to dry if he saw him like this. A drop of sweat dripped off his nose.

Mark pictured the headlines: Partner of Prestigious Atlanta Law Firm Found Buck-Naked In Men's-Room Stall Amidst Pile of Women's Underthings. He could visualize himself saying, "Honest, Officer, I was just loaning my clothes to my fake fiancée's transvestite roommate so the senior partner of my law firm wouldn't find out I'd set him up with a man."

Specklemeyer's feet had disappeared, and Mark prayed the man would simply leave. He nearly had a stroke when he heard a gasp above him. Mark turned and looked straight up into his co-worker's astonished face hanging over the top of the stall.

"Blackwell?" he screeched, his voice incredulous.

Mark reached up to grab him by the throat, dropping most of the clothing he held. "Listen, you jackass, this isn't what you think, and if you so much as breathe a word of this to anyone, I'll rip out your spleen, got it?"

But Specklemeyer wasn't shaken. "Gee, Blackwell, you're much more intimidating when you're not wielding a pair of size eleven turquoise pumps."

Mark looked down at the shoe in his other hand. His fury exploded, and he shook the man until his head rattled. His voice was low and deadly. "I mean it, Specklemeyer. You did not see this."

Tony held up his hands in surrender and rolled a smile around on his lips. "Sure, man, sure. Whatever you say." He jerked loose from Mark's grip, and Mark heard him step down from the toilet seat and leave the rest room.

Mark sank to the toilet and put his face in his hands. *My career is definitely over.* Next week, being partner would be a distant memory.

He clasped his hands together. "Please, God, let me get out of here alive so I can wring Ellie Sutherland's neck!"

ELLIE HELPED an unsteady Ray into his seat before she slid into hers. She glanced around frantically for Manny and Mark. They'd been gone for several minutes.

"I need to visit the men's room," Ray announced, half standing.

"No!" Ellie yelled, drawing the attention of patrons around her.

Ray looked at her, startled.

"I mean, not yet," she said, laughing nervously. "Can you wait until Mark or Molly get back so I won't be here by myself?"

Ray sat back down obligingly. "Where *are* those two?"

Good question.

"Ellie!" Manny's voice exclaimed behind her. She turned to see Manny, clad in Mark's clothing, striding toward her. Despite her panic, she had to suppress a giggle. His feet were swimming in the bigger man's shoes, and he'd rolled up the cuff of the dress pants to keep them from dragging.

"Where's Molly?" Manny asked dramatically.

"I think she's in the ladies' room, Manny."

"Is this a friend of yours, Ellie?" Ray asked cautiously.

"Ray Ivan, meet Manny Oliver."

Ray stuck out his hand, perplexed. "Pleased to meet you."

Manny didn't shake his hand, and instead cried, "Are you the man who's trying to steal my Molly?"

"What?" the older man exclaimed.

Manny swooped down on one knee and clasped Ray's hands. "Don't do it, sir. If you have a heart, don't do it."

"Don't do what?" Concern lined Ray's face.

"Don't take my Molly." Big tears filled Manny's eyes. "I love her, but she keeps a flock of men on the side. She's so beautiful, I can't compete with them all. You understand, don't you, sir?"

"I guess so," Ray said dubiously.

Ellie hid a smile behind her napkin. Manny hadn't removed his eyelashes, and his long fingernails were still blood red, but the sodden Ray didn't seem to notice.

The maître d' approached the table with a worried look on his face. He addressed Ray. "Is everything all right here, sir?"

Manny's sobs increased, his head bent over Ray's hands.

"I think so," Ray said in confusion.

Manny raised his head. "So you'll give me your word to not see her, no matter how tempting she is."

Ray looked at Ellie, then back to Manny. "I guess so."

"Oh, thank you, sir." Manny's sobs began anew. "You've made me a new man. But please, when she comes back out, let her down gently. I love her so much, I couldn't stand for her to be hurt."

Ray nodded rapidly. "Sure."

Manny kissed the man's hands, then made a tearful exit.

"I'm so sorry, Ray," Ellie said, patting his hand. "Perhaps it really is for the best."

He nodded wisely. "Better to have loved and lost..." His voice faded as he lifted his wineglass to his lips for the hundredth time.

A few minutes later, Mark came walking hurriedly back to the table, glancing around the room and tugging at his tie.

"Where've you been?" Ray slurred. "We've been worried about you, son."

Mark glared murderously at Ellie, but turned a smile on Ray. "The snails didn't agree with me, sir."

"Have you seen Molly?" Ellie asked, her eyebrows raised.

"I believe she'll be here any minute," he said through clenched teeth.

"Hello, all," Manny said in his sugary Molly voice, swinging into his seat.

He looked slightly worse for wear, his wig askew and lipstick hastily applied. He turned a smile on Ray. "Miss me?"

"Yes," Ray admitted, his voice sad. "But I'm afraid I must call it an evening."

"But why?" Manny's eyebrows furrowed dramatically.

Ray took Manny's hand in his. "Well, the truth is, Molly, you're too much of a woman for me, and I don't think this is going to work out."

"Oh, no." Manny pouted prettily.

Mark rolled his eyes, and Ellie kicked him under the table.

"Shush, my dear," Ray said gently. "It's for the best. You've been a lovely dinner companion, and I thank you very much."

''Well, if you're sure,'' Manny said cautiously.

Ray waved for the maître d' and asked him to hail a taxi, then signed for the meal, folded a fifty into the man's hand and bid everyone good-night.

When he was out of sight, Ellie sank into her chair in relief. ''Whew!''

Manny snapped his fingers. ''Told you it would work.''

''Except,'' she added glumly, ''he still thinks we're engaged.''

Mark scanned the room again, obviously agitated. His scowl was black and ugly when it landed on Ellie. ''Although being engaged to you is a harrowing prospect, believe me, it's the least of my problems right now.''

FREDA ESCORTED ELLIE to the first available closet-room. ''So,'' the clinical assistant said in a tired voice. ''How's it going?'' She sat down heavily in a creaking metal chair and flipped through Ellie's journal, stopping occasionally to scratch at her temple with the end of a pen.

''Fine,'' Ellie replied nervously, sitting on a stool wedged between a trash can and a Formica desk. Absolutely nothing in her life was fine.

Freda had stopped on one page to read intently. ''Well, I can see things have progressed nicely with Mr. Mark.''

''Keep reading,'' Ellie said dryly.

Freda squinted, bringing the book closer. ''Try to remember to print your entries next time.''

''But I printed them *this* time.''

''Well, it's hard to make out what you've written. You had 'toy' sex? Is that something new?''

Ellie felt her skin redden. She coughed lightly. ''Mmm, that would be 'toe' sex.''

''*Toe* sex? Okay, you had, er...*toe* sex once and regular sex once?''

''That's right.''

Freda studied a form on her desk, pen poised, then shook her head. ''I never seem to have the right checkboxes for your answers.''

"Being categorized under 'other' is the story of my life."

"Do you see this moving toward a long-term relationship?"

"Definitely not."

Freda kept writing. "How often do you see him?"

"For the next few weeks, possibly every day—I work out of his home now, but it's temporary, and partly so I can look after my cat."

"He's keeping your cat?"

"Uh-huh."

"But last week you told me he's allergic to your cat."

"He is, but we made this deal he'd look after her until she had kittens if I would go to a swanky work dinner party as his date. Except it didn't go very well because his partner caught us making out in the car and then announced to everyone that we're engaged."

Freda's eyes widened. "You're engaged?"

"No, but everyone thinks so. Except his mom—he told her the truth because she nearly had a heart attack when she heard it through the grapevine. She hates me because I—"

"Ruined the family reunion," Freda cut in. "You told me."

"It was an accident," Ellie insisted. "Then we double-dated with his partner and my roommate, only Mark didn't know my roommate is a transvestite—"

"Wait," Freda said, holding her palm stop-sign fashion. "That's a whole different study. Let's get back to the pheromones. Have you had sex since you started working in his home?"

"He's not speaking to me."

"Because of the roommate?"

Ellie nodded. "It's a long story, but a co-worker of Mark's saw him in the bathroom naked and holding a bunch of women's clothes—"

"Wait, I thought your roommate was the cross-dresser."

"He is."

Freda looked at her questioningly. "Then why was Mark naked in the bathroom holding women's clothes?"

"He had to loan *his* clothes to my roommate to convince

his partner that the woman he thought he was with had a boyfriend.''

Freda looked totally confused. ''And that boyfriend would be...?''

''My roommate.''

Pursing her lips, Freda said, ''Okay.''

''Anyway, Mark hasn't spoken to me since he dropped me and my roommate off Saturday night.''

''I thought you said you were working in his home.''

''But I only started yesterday. He worked late, probably on purpose, and I left before he got home.''

''Why don't you stick around one night until he comes home and see what happens?'' She winked, surprising Ellie. ''See how long he can resist you.''

''The problem is, these pheromones seem to be working both ways.''

''What do you mean?''

''Why else would I be so drawn to a man who is everything I would hate in a partner? It has to be these pills.''

''Probably,'' Freda agreed, nodding. Spreading her hands, she added, ''Think of it as one big science project.''

''Oh, no,'' Ellie groaned.

''What?''

''I blew up the science lab my junior year in college.''

9

WHY, oh, why had he ever thought he'd be able to resist her, and in his own home, no less? Purposely working late each night, Mark half hoped she'd be gone when he arrived, half prayed she wouldn't be. Tonight was Friday and his prayers had been answered. Classic rock thumped through his centralized stereo system when he stepped into the entryway. He inhaled, filling his lungs with her fresh-air skin scent that had permeated his home.

"Ellie," he called, and although he knew she couldn't hear him above Lynyrd Skynyrd, he added, "I'm home." For a few foolish seconds, the image of an aproned June Cleaver flashed through his mind, coming to the door to welcome Ward home from a hard day's work.

"Mark, is that you?" Ellie bawled, coming to the top of the stairs to peer over the railing.

Except June had never worn an apron like that, he mused, admiring the way the short work smock emphasized Ellie's breasts and small waist. And Mrs. Cleaver would have been holding a spatula instead of a paintbrush.

Mark waved, deciding not to yell over the music. He hated himself for being so glad to see her. She held up a finger to indicate she'd be back, then disappeared. Mark set his briefcase by the bottom step and loosened his tie. Walking toward the kitchen, he bellowed, "How have you been?" His last two words reverberated through the house because the music abruptly ended. Then he heard the sound of Ellie's feet descending the stairs lightly and rhythmically.

"Oh, fine," she said cheerfully.

When he turned to her, he noticed immediately she'd lost

the smock. Black hip-hugger shorts and a ribbed lime green turtleneck would have been unforgivable on most women, but Ellie, as usual, looked delightful. Right down to the smudge of gold paint on her chin. Then he realized her cheer had been forced. Her wide smile could not hide her bright, panicked eyes. He slowly placed the two bottles of beer he'd withdrawn from the refrigerator on the counter. "What?" he asked, alarm setting in.

"You might want to have something stronger than a beer," she warned.

Mark bit his lip and summoned patience. "What?" he repeated quietly.

Ellie's face took on a pleading look. "She's just a sweet little kitty, Mark, please don't be mad."

Mark snorted and twisted off the beer cap. "What did Sheba do today? Pee on another blue cushion?"

He lifted the bottle to his mouth, but stopped at the look of dread on Ellie's face. Obviously this was much worse than a couple of throw pillows. "What did she break?"

"She didn't break anything, exactly."

"What the hell did she do, *exactly?*" Suddenly Mark realized the buzz from his fish-tank filter was absent. His head jerked around. "Oh, no. Not my fish?"

Ellie stood wringing her hands. "I guess the fish video got her wound up—"

Anger bubbled inside his stomach. "Your cat *ate* my fish?"

She bit her bottom lip, then said, "Well, she didn't eat *all* of them, mostly just batted them around—"

Mark strode through the kitchen into the den to stare at the fifty-gallon tank of serene, still water. Artificial sea grass drifted up from the bottom. A labyrinth of elaborate ceramic sand castles sat vacant. A single black severed fish tail floated on the surface.

"I turned off the filter," she offered. "And sang 'The Circle of Life' when I flushed them down the john."

"At that point, I'm sure they were glad to be dead," Mark retorted, remembering her singing voice. "What happened to the lid?"

''The veterinarian says Esmerelda has an above average IQ—''

Mark cut her off. ''If that were the case, the animal would be smart enough to know not to devour seven hundred dollars' worth of exotic fish!''

Ellie blanched. ''Seven hundred dollars? Are you crazy? That's two months' rent.''

Mark narrowed his eyes.

Smiling nervously, Ellie quietly stammered, ''Well, you certainly can't f-fault her good taste.''

Irritation triggered a finger twitch. Soon his hands were jumping at his sides. ''I'm filling it up with piranhas tomorrow.'' He strode back to the kitchen, gulped half the beer, then added, ''Big, smart piranhas that say, 'Here, kitty, kitty.'''

''I'm sorry, Mark, really I am, and I know Esmerelda is sorry, too, if only she could tell you,'' she pleaded, hot on his heels.

''Oh, so *that's* what she's trying to say when she bares her fangs and runs me out of my own bed.''

''Please, Mark,'' Ellie begged softly. When he turned, she slipped inside the circle of his arms. Desire bolted through him against his will. Wrapping her arms around his waist, she turned huge blue eyes up to him, batting her lashes shamelessly. ''She's going to be a mother in a couple of weeks,'' she said earnestly, as if that explained everything.

''Meow,'' Esmerelda announced, walking regally into the room, tail held high. She glanced toward the den and licked her lips, then blinked at Mark.

''Long live the queen,'' Mark grumbled, but set his beer down to draw Ellie closer to him.

Ellie inhaled sharply when he tightened his hold. Her breasts, without the protection of a bra, responded immediately. Mark's voice was low as he lowered his mouth to her ear. ''If you think kissing up to me is going to make up for that murdering cat of yours, well, then—''

She moved her lips to his and drew his breath into her mouth with a slow, deep kiss.

When she withdrew, he simply stared down at her. "Well, then...you're much smarter than your pussycat." He shook his head in wonder. "Between last weekend and my empty aquarium, I should be furious with you."

"But?" she asked hopefully.

"But...there's something about you that makes me forget what I was feeling or saying before you walked into the room," he said, hearing the wonder in his own voice.

Ellie's smile was tremulous. "I'm sorry. I should have told you about Manny. Does his cross-dressing bother you?"

Mark thought about it for a few seconds. "No. I mean, it takes a little getting used to, but he seems like an okay guy." He smiled wryly. "I just didn't want to be the one who paired him up with the man who respected me enough to make me a partner."

She played with a buttonhole in his jacket. "So did you get in trouble for...you know."

"For my stint as a naked clothes rack for your friend?"

She giggled and nodded.

He loosened his grip on her waist, took a drink of his beer and leaned against the counter. "Specklemeyer hasn't come out and said anything, but he's flirting with disaster."

"How so?"

"We had a meeting this morning with an old client, and Ray told him I was engaged." He watched her expression, curious for a reaction, perplexed by his own curiosity. Her face remained unreadable, and he continued, "I opened my mouth to set the record straight, but Tony sat gloating across the table. He really thinks I'm covering up some kind of kinky life-style. I figured telling everyone we're not engaged would only add fuel to his fire. I'm sorry to keep prolonging this."

She shrugged, a smile on her lips. "Do you think he'll say anything?"

"If I know Specklemeyer, he'll wait until he needs my support for something big, then he'll threaten to tell what he thinks he saw."

"Is he that vicious?"

"He's so blinded by ambition, I wouldn't put anything past

him. The man has a vanity license plate that says 'HUNGRY.'"

"Would they really fire you?"

"Of course not—even if I were a cross-dresser, it would be illegal to fire me. But it's a label I'd rather not have to defend." God, she smelled wonderful. He pulled her to him and kissed her neck. She felt dangerously good and his body hardened in need. No, his mind screamed, a thousand times no. "Do you have dinner plans?" he asked, nuzzling her ear.

She pressed her breasts against him, moaning slightly. "Nothing I can't get out of," she whispered. "What did you have in mind?"

"Getting you out of something," he murmured, ignoring the warning bells in his head. "Do you think Esmerelda would let us borrow my room for the night? I still haven't seen that darn tattoo."

ELLIE SAT UP GINGERLY so as not to disturb Mark, her heart catching at the sight of him sprawled in the tangled sheets. They'd made love, then ordered Ellie's favorite ham and pineapple pizza, washed it down with beer and made love again. He'd asked her to accompany him to a regatta today in Savannah, and she was looking forward to spending the day together. It seemed he did have time for rest and relaxation, after all. Maybe he wasn't the work machine she had imagined.

At the moment, she sincerely doubted if even Esmerelda could rouse the man. Mark's soft snores attested to his deep state of sleep, but it was his state of undress that mesmerized Ellie. She studied the proportion of his torso, the hard planes of his stomach and the length of his semihard sex with an artist's trained eye. On impulse, she began to frame a composition with her joined thumbs and extended index fingers. Some scenes were meant to be captured on paper. Mark Blackwell in the buff was an artist's dream.

Silently, Ellie rose and lifted his blue-and-white-striped pajama top from the bedpost, then pulled it over her head. She rolled up the sleeves and padded to Esmerelda's room where she had set up an easel and paints.

The corporate portrait was progressing nicely. Mark was coming alive on the canvas surface, devastatingly masculine and authoritative in his olive suit. She'd coaxed him into sitting for her last night in the few minutes between their lovemaking sessions, and had taken advantage of the time to render his eyes. This most important feature was most accurately portrayed if painted directly from the model in order to capture light and expression. They glistened back at her, serious, but with a teasing twinkle at the edges. Volumes of dark leather-bound reference books made up the background, the books' gilded accents a perfect foil for the green in his suit and eyes.

Ellie snatched her large sketch pad and flipped past the quick sketches of Esmerelda until she found a clean sheet. Then she reentered Mark's bedroom, sighing when Esmerelda dashed through the door before she could close it. Mark remained deep in slumber. She'd bet he hadn't so much as twitched since she'd left.

Sinking into an overstuffed chair in front of the bay window, Ellie propped her feet on an ottoman and spent a few seconds drinking in the sight of Mark's glorious body. The thick charcoal pencil in her hand began to move almost involuntarily. Within minutes she'd scrawled a rough sketch of him across the page. On the second pass, she worked more slowly, blocking in shadows to delineate limbs and muscles. Finally, she added more detail, like body hair and facial features. Taking particular care, she rendered his privates in precise proportion on the paper. Not hard, yet not soft, his current state of semiarousal would aptly reflect his size, yet not come across as vulgar.

The sketch turned out so well, Ellie decided a painting must be done. She grinned. It would be her unique thank-you to Mark for taking care of Esmerelda. He'd probably get a big kick out of it. What man hadn't fantasized about being immortalized in the nude at the peak of health? She'd work on the new painting at her apartment to keep it a secret.

She closed the sketchbook and put it aside to crawl back into bed. Mark grunted contentedly when she spooned up next to him. *I can't believe I'm so stupid. I fell in love with him knowing full well he's devoted to his job. I promised myself I'd never get tied to a man who thought being with his family was an option. Besides, the study ends in two weeks, along with my sex appeal.*

The phone rang, jarring Mark awake. Ellie reached for the handset on the nightstand and gave it to him. He pulled himself up, rubbing the sleep from his eyes, and spoke into the phone. "Hello? Yeah, Patrick...no, I'm fine, what's up?" Mark reached for the pen and pad beside the phone and began to jot down notes. "No, I'll be glad to take care of it." He glanced at Ellie and frowned apologetically. "Have Monica make the arrangements and clear my calendar for next week. I'll be at the airport in forty-five minutes." He was already standing when he hung up the phone.

"Sorry about today," he said simply, tearing off the sheet of paper. "Something came up—I have to go to Chicago with Beecham and Ivan for a week or so." He bent over and kissed her quickly.

Déjà vu. How many times had her father missed planned outings with the family because his boss had called at the last minute? "Oh, come on, can't you wait until this afternoon?" Ellie cajoled.

Mark shook his head. "Sorry, I have a plane to catch. Grant was supposed to go but had to cancel at the last minute. That leaves me."

"Can't we at least have breakfast?" Ellie pleaded, hating herself for sounding like her mother.

"Sorry," he repeated. "I'll make it up to you when I get home. I promise." Then he walked toward the bathroom. After he closed the door and the shower spray started, Ellie frowned and pounded her fist on the mattress.

Sorry, sorry, sorry. Her father had had an endless supply of apologies. Rising from the bed, she scooped her clothing from the floor. She cursed under her breath, and shook her head. She had no one to blame but herself. She'd seen the train coming, but had barreled past the warning signals to straddle the tracks, welcoming the light with open arms.

SATURDAY AND SUNDAY NIGHT had both been late work nights in Chicago. And since what little sleep time he'd had left he'd spent thinking about Ellie, Mark arrived at the hotel's continental breakfast Monday morning in a less-than-rested mood.

He couldn't get the woman off his mind. Of course, the irritating rash he'd developed from the foamy whipped cream she'd covered his privates with served as a constant reminder of their romps. Granted, she had removed it in a most satisfying way. *It's just a strong physical attraction.* Unfortunately, the one area in which they seemed to be most compatible was in bed.

He purposely hadn't called her since he'd left. Somehow, calling long distance to check in just seemed too...relationship-y. Still, the idea of spending a lot of time with Ellie had begun to sound appealing. The mere thought of the tiny pink mouse tattoo, apparently barely concealed by her garter belt that first night, sent the blood rushing to his groin. Ellie was beautiful, sexy, funny, and he craved her company. He could do much worse, he knew. He might give this novel idea of a committed, monogamous relationship some serious thought.

"How's Ellie?" Patrick asked, breaking into his thoughts.

Mark glanced at Ray, who also seemed interested in his answer. For an instant, Mark wondered if Specklemeyer had leaked the information, after all. Maybe they knew his engagement was a charade and were calling him on it. Shifting in his seat, he replied, "Fine, thanks for asking."

Patrick looked sympathetic. "Big step, isn't it?"

Mark nodded, swallowing a dry bite of bagel.

"Of course it's a big step," Ray declared, snapping open a newspaper. "The last woman you'll sleep with for the rest of your life, the one woman you'll wake up to every day for the next fifty years, God willing."

Patrick nodded solemnly. "Of course, the bedroom gets a little chilly once kids come along, but you get used to it."

Ray grunted his agreement. "Bone-cold."

Mark pursed his lips and shook his head, smiling wryly.

"So why don't married men reveal this stuff to single men *before* the engagement?"

Ray chuckled. "We're not trying to talk you out of it, son. Marriage has its good points. If the right woman came along, I'd do it again." He rattled the newspaper. "Probably." Mark thought about Manny and winced.

"Yeah," Patrick said, "Lucy is fabulous, it's her mother I can't stomach. By the way, how's your mother taking this?"

"She's not ecstatic, but—"

"Uh-oh," Ivan announced from behind the paper. "Not a good sign, but it's to be expected. Don't worry, things will probably work out before one of your parents has to move in."

"Move in?" Mark parroted.

"Sure," Patrick said. "After Lucy's father passed away, her mother was so heavily medicated, she came to stay with us for a couple of weeks. She's been living with us going on two years now."

Mark swallowed. He doubted he could live with his *own* mother, and he didn't know the first thing about Ellie's family. Except that her dad had been a workaholic. But hadn't she said something about a nudist colony? His collar grew warmer and tighter.

"That's nothing," said Ray, bending down a corner of a page to peer at them. "My mother came to live with us back in 1970. She and my poor wife argued so much, the police were at my house three times the first week because the neighbors complained."

Mark imagined his mother and Ellie in the same house. Not in a million years. He pushed his plate away and grabbed a glass of water. He'd never experienced heartburn before, but it didn't take a medical degree to perform a quick diagnosis. His previous notion of entering a relationship with Ellie ended along with his appetite.

10

ELLIE WAVED at the messy painters as she ducked through the entryway of the clinic. She was almost sorry she wouldn't be around to see the finished product.

Freda stood behind the receptionist's counter when Ellie walked in. "Well, if it isn't the woman with the experienced toes." The woman's eyes were actually twinkling. She led Ellie back to a tiny room and asked, "So, what's the latest?"

"Nothing kinky this week," Ellie informed her as she took a seat and handed her the journal. "I consider whipped cream to be pretty standard stuff."

"Oh?"

"We were together Friday night, then he left town Saturday."

"Sounds like he came around."

Ellie grinned sheepishly. "Around and around and upside down."

Showing uncharacteristic concern, Freda asked, "Have you heard from him?"

Ellie shook her head sadly. "It's the pheromones, isn't it? He's not near me to be affected by them, so he's not interested."

"Is that what you think?" Freda asked, her pen poised.

Ellie nodded.

"Could be," Freda admitted, making notes. "But haven't you heard the saying 'Absence makes the heart grow fonder'?"

"I thought it was 'Absence make the heart wonder.' Or is it 'wander'?"

"You don't have much confidence in your relationship, do you?"

Ellie's laugh was short and dry. "Relationship? What Mark and I have is a physical attraction brought about by these...these fake love-inducers." She pointed to the bottle of pills sitting in front of Freda. "It's not fair—they mess with a person's mind—they make you think something's there that really isn't." She blinked away tears and tried to smile at Freda. "Tennyson was wrong—it's better *not* to have loved at all than to have loved and lost."

"You haven't lost him yet," Freda said.

"Yeah," Ellie said miserably, gesturing to her final supply. "This should delay the inevitable by about one week."

"Have you considered the possibility you might feel differently about *him* once you quit taking the pills?"

Elation zigged, then zagged through Ellie's heart. She lifted her chin and flashed a genuine smile in Freda's direction. "You're right!" A burden the size of Mark's cellular phone bill rolled off her back. Since it was a chemically induced fluke she'd fallen for the very type of man she'd sworn to avoid, this attraction would probably disappear as quickly as it had surfaced.

"Anyway," Freda said, "it'll be interesting to see what happens when he returns." She handed Ellie the final week's supply of pheromones.

Ellie fingered the bottle, the pills suddenly weighing heavily in her palm. The honeymoon was almost over, and she was happy to see the end in sight.

Wasn't she?

"WHERE HAVE YOU been keeping yourself?" Manny asked, dumping his bags of groceries on the counter. "As if I didn't know," he added.

Ellie angled her head at him across the room. She'd set up an easel in a corner of the breakfast nook by the window. After wiping a brush on a turpentine-soaked rag, she stretched her cramped fingers. Sometimes, a picture practically painted itself. This was one of those times when once she started painting, she couldn't bring herself to stop. She checked her watch. Three hours, nonstop.

Manny walked over to peek at the painting and gasped, his hand to his chest. "My, my." Mark Blackwell lay slumbering on the canvas, his sleek and muscled nude body accented, not covered, by the twisted sheets. "Now I know where the phrase *too big for his britches* originated."

"Manny," Ellie warned, "if you let on you've seen this painting, I swear I'll burn your gowns."

With his hand, Manny made a zipping motion across his mouth, then turned back to the painting. "It's divine, El," he said with sincerity in his voice.

"One of my best," she agreed. "A shame no one will ever see it."

"Then why on earth did you paint it?"

"It's a surprise gift to Mark for taking care of Esmerelda."

Manny looked incredulous. "He doesn't know about it?"

"Nope."

"Well, that explains a few things. I thought it was rather loose of Mr. A. Retentive. How's the other painting going?"

"Almost finished. Mark's in Chicago."

"When did he leave?"

"Saturday morning."

"This is Tuesday. You've been at his house three entire days by yourself?"

"Esmerelda was there," Ellie said defensively.

"What have you been doing?"

"Working on the other portrait, weeding his flowers—"

"Sleeping in his bed. Did you rearrange the furniture, too, Goldilocks?"

"No! Although the couch in his den *would* look better under the window."

"You're getting too comfortable at this house," Manny warned. "What's going on with the two of you?"

"That's a very good question."

"And?"

"And I intend to pursue an answer once he returns from his trip."

"Which will be?"

"Soon, I think."

By Friday, when she still hadn't heard from Mark, Ellie was decidedly depressed. Pride kept her from calling his office to see when they expected him to return. She'd put the final touches on the business portrait still drying at his home. The finished nude, drying on an easel in her bedroom, no longer seemed like such a grand idea.

Mark Blackwell was firmly entrenched in his career, and had made it crystal clear this week he didn't care enough about her to spare five minutes of his busy schedule to call. For all she knew, he could be flitting around the Windy City with a busty woman on each arm. In fact, the more she dwelled on it, the more convinced she became he was doing just that. Misery wallowed in her stomach.

Saturday afternoon, Ellie returned home with new sketches for two more Atlanta landmark paintings she intended to add to her portfolio. A quick glance at her answering machine told her there was one message. Her heart lifted. Mark? She rushed over to the machine and pushed the play button.

"Ellie, this is Monica. I wanted to let you know in case Mark hasn't called that he'll be back Wednesday morning." So, she'd been relegated to receiving messages through his secretary, and probably only because Monica had taken it upon herself to forward the information. She knew the routine—some weeks her mother had talked to her husband's secretary more than she'd spoken to her own husband.

Ellie's heart crumbled in disappointment. She deserved more than a philandering businessman who slept with his briefcase. More than a man who would fly off for weeks at a time and never check in. She refused to expose herself to it, she refused to expose her children to it. Ellie made a painful decision. If Mark Blackwell ever came home, she wouldn't be seeing him anymore. Which was just as well, she noted. The end of the study loomed in plain sight.

She went to the Dunwoody house that afternoon to check on Esmerelda, and decided from the looks of her cat's bulging tummy, she'd better start spending the nights again, at least until Mark came home. To soothe her guilty pangs, Ellie slept in a guest room and bought groceries, then puttered around the yard, weeding, watering, trimming, even transplanting. She found a tiny vacant mulch bed which would have made a perfect herb garden, but she swept the thought aside. Better to concentrate on reality, such as finding a job.

So the next morning, she and Esmerelda pored over Mark's Sunday-paper classified ads. She would receive the last check from the study on Tuesday when she turned in her final journal, which was practically blank this week, except for the occasional street admirer. She'd be able to collect the largest and final installment on Mark's portrait from the law firm in a couple of weeks. But she needed to look for something steady and, preferably, with insurance.

Ellie sighed, circling possibilities, tears filling her eyes when she remembered the last time she'd done this. It had been the day Mark Blackwell had bumbled his way into her life. Only this time, tears, not displaced soda, wet the paper. Ellie wished she'd never heard of pheromones, because if not for those darned pills, she wouldn't have lost her heart to Mark. She put her head down and cried in earnest. Esmerelda licked Ellie's hand.

IF ELLIE HAD ANY DOUBTS about whether she wore her heart on her sleeve, Freda put them to rest Tuesday morning.

"I take it he's still in Chicago?"

Ellie nodded forlornly.

"And you haven't heard from him?"

She shook her head, just as forlornly.

"When is he due back?"

"His secretary left me a message he'll be back tomorrow."

"And you'll be taking your last two pills this evening, right?"

Ellie nodded again.

Freda sighed. "Don't fret about it—you'll just make yourself sick." She smiled and patted Ellie's hand. "Good luck."

"WHAT'S THE PROBLEM?" Mark grumbled to Patrick. They'd been sitting on a runway at O'Hare for over forty minutes waiting for their plane to take off.

Patrick looked up from his magazine. "Relax, man, this is typical."

"You think they could at least serve us a beer while we wait."

Patrick raised an eyebrow. "Are you cranky for a particular reason or can I look forward to this every time we fly together?"

Mark frowned. "Sorry."

His partner laughed. "Hey, I miss Lucy, too. You'll be home before you know it. And reunion sex is the best, don't you think? It's the only time I can get near Lucy anymore." He went back to his reading, leaving Mark to brood.

He'd decided earlier in the week he wouldn't be seeing Ellie anymore. That is, he wouldn't be *dating* her anymore. She'd still be at his house occasionally during the next few weeks until that darn cat dropped her kittens and weaned them. Come to think of it, he and Ellie hadn't really dated much, when he subtracted the dates he'd bartered for and the disastrous double date with Ray and Manny.

Okay, so he wouldn't be *sleeping* with her anymore. That thought sent a pang of regret through his midsection, but he remained determined. He was too young to settle down and when he did, it would be to someone better suited for him. He hadn't figured out the hold she seemed to have over him, but if staying away from Ellie and her powerful sex appeal held the answer, he'd do it. He'd made sacrifices before. He'd be happier in the long run. So how to break the news to her? The way men had been delivering bad news for decades. In the gentlest, safest way possible.

By telephone.

ELLIE'S HEART LEAPED involuntarily at the sound of the ringing phone. Manny's eyes shot up in question as he reached for the handset. She motioned for him to answer it.

"Hello? Yes, she is. May I ask who's calling? Well, Mark,

how nice of you to call. We thought you'd died. Hold on, please."

Ellie rolled her eyes.

Manny covered the mouthpiece and said unnecessarily, "It's him."

After taking several deep breaths to calm herself, Ellie picked up the handset and said, "Hello?"

"Hi, it's Mark."

She couldn't read anything into the tone of his voice. But he didn't sound especially glad to be talking to her. "Oh, hi. Are you home?"

"Yeah."

"How was your trip?" She tried to shoo Manny from the room with her hand, but he smiled and shook his head, plopping down on the couch within hearing distance.

"I had a busy week," Mark said distractedly. "And long. It'll be nice to sleep in my own bed tonight."

The silence hung heavy after his loaded offhand comment.

Ellie cleared her throat. "Well, hopefully Esmerelda won't bother you."

"I see she still hasn't had her kittens."

"No, but she should any day. I hope you don't mind—I stayed over there the last few nights in case she needed me."

"So you're the one who replenished my beer."

"Yeah, I figured it was the least I could do. I can't tell you how much I appreciate your letting her stay." She was rambling, she knew, but she wasn't sure where they stood anymore.

"A deal's a deal," he said simply. "The portrait looks finished." He seemed to be grasping at conversational straws, too.

"It is. As soon as the paint is dry enough, I'll bring it home to frame."

"Would it sound conceited if I said it looked great?"

"A little, but I know what you mean. Thanks."

"Sure." He cleared his throat. "Look, Ellie, I've been thinking now would be a good time to let everyone at work know our engagement is, well...off."

Ellie bit her bottom lip to stem her tears. Although she'd been entertaining the same thoughts, it just sounded so final coming from his mouth. Manny leaned forward on the couch, looking ready to pounce on the phone. She took a deep, steadying breath. "Uh, sure, my thoughts exactly. I'm sure no one will be surprised. We're not really each other's type, you know."

"Right." He sounded relieved. "But, hey, don't let that keep you away. I know you'll be wanting to check on Esmerelda, so hang on to that key, okay?"

"Okay," she said, forcing brightness into her voice.

"I'll see you soon, then?"

"Soon," she promised, and hung up slowly. When she turned, Manny was already by her side. He pulled her into his arms, rocking her and shushing her tears.

AFTER UNPACKING and showering, Mark went to the office for a few hours, but couldn't seem to concentrate. *I'm tired,* he rationalized. He toyed with the idea of calling Valerie, but an early evening and a long night's rest sounded more appealing. He carefully kept at bay the words and emotions of this morning's stilted phone conversation with Ellie. In a few weeks, he'd forget about her. He'd probably run into her one day with a rumpled poet on her arm. He frowned, then pushed all thoughts of Ellie Sutherland from his mind.

After pulling into the garage, Mark walked back down his short driveway to check the mailbox. While idly flipping through bills and junk mail, he scrutinized his landscaping. Something seemed different, but he couldn't put his finger on it. Not one thing, but maybe everything. He stopped. The gardens were neater, perhaps. Which was odd, since the landscaping company wasn't scheduled to come out for another month. He examined the bushes and flowers more closely. Completely weed free. And showing evidence of recent pruning. Frowning, he reentered the garage, then noticed his gardening gloves were hung in a different spot. As were some of his tools. Ellie? He shook his head, a small smile curving his lips.

All was quiet when he entered the house. For a split second he craved Lynyrd Skynyrd, but settled on a shot of bourbon. After he poured the drink, he stopped to study the expensive crystal decanter, heavy and cool in his hands. Very elegant, like all his possessions. Given the chance, how would Ellie spend his money? Leopard-skin-upholstered furniture? Baubles for the cat?

Trudging upstairs to change, Mark registered the fact that Esmerelda hadn't made her normal snooty appearance. Probably lying in wait somewhere to pounce on him, he decided. He walked into his bedroom, flipping on the light. He reached for the remote and tuned in a sports channel, then stripped off his clothes as he walked through the bathroom and into his walk-in closet to retrieve a pair of sweats. A slow, low growl sounded beneath the spot his long coats were hanging.

"Out of here, Esmerelda," Mark said sternly, moving the coats aside to shoo her away. A pungent, sweet odor reached his nostrils an instant before his first sneeze. Never fond of seeing blood, Mark noted it seemed especially graphic against the light camel of his best cashmere coat. "Nope, can't fault your good taste," he muttered, allowing the coats to fall gently back into place as he backed out of the closet, and trotted to the phone.

Manny answered it on the second ring.

"Hello?"

"Is Ellie there?"

"She's not feeling very well. Who's this?"

Mark sighed in frustration. "It's Mark. I need to talk to Ellie about her cat. There's blood everywhere."

"SHE'LL BE FINE, you'll see," Manny assured her. He'd insisted on accompanying Ellie because she felt so ill.

The rhythm of the train threatened to lull Ellie's mind to numbness. She knew she looked like hell. Passengers averted their eyes. Between the crying jags and a head cold she'd succumbed to this evening, she felt as if she'd been trampled. Her eyes were red and puffy, her nose the size of W. C.

Fields's. She sneezed savagely into a large crumpled handkerchief.

"Your immunity is down," Manny chided. "All that worrying over a straight man, for heaven's sake."

Ellie felt too miserable to respond. Her chest ached. And to cap off this rotten day, Mark would see her at her absolute worst. Then he'd be kicking his heels he'd broken it off.

"You shouldn't have come," Manny mumbled.

"Esmerelda needs me," she managed to get out between parched lips. It hurt to breathe.

"*You* need you. That cat can take care of herself."

"Manny—"

"Okay, okay, I'll hush."

Mark stood waiting for her when they stepped off the train. She tried to calm the beating of her heart, but it raced at the sight of him. A look of concern came over him when she drew nearer.

"Are you okay?" he asked.

"No," Manny snapped. "I couldn't talk her out of coming."

"It's just a cold," Ellie assured them, blowing her nose noisily. "How's Esmerelda?"

"In labor, as far as I could tell," Mark said, studying her. "Maybe you should go home."

"No, I want to see her. Manny offered to meet me here in two hours, if you don't mind bringing me back."

He touched her elbow and steered her in the direction of his car. "You'll stay at my place tonight," he said firmly. Then at the look of challenge on Manny's face, he added, "In a guest room."

"El?" Manny asked, apparently not ready to relinquish her to Mark's care.

"I'll call you later," she promised.

The short trip to Mark's home was silent, punctuated only by Ellie's occasional sneeze or cough. Her arms ached to touch him, or just plain ached, she couldn't tell which. When they arrived, Ellie asked, "Where is she?"

"In my closet."

She made her way up the stairs as quickly as her complaining joints would allow, Mark following her wordlessly. Esmerelda's deep purr could be heard at the top of the stairs. Ellie rushed to the closet and gently pushed back the coats. In the dim light from the bathroom, the proud mother lay on her side with her new kittens gathered around.

"Oh, Esmerelda," she said softly. "You're a mother, five times over." The cat raised her head weakly at Ellie's voice, then closed her eyes to rest. "Look at them," Ellie whispered in awe. The tiny wet balls of fur resembled hamsters, wriggling next to their mama.

"Tiny, aren't they?" Mark asked over her shoulder. Ellie stood and turned to him. "I'm sorry about your coat. I'll pay for it, and the fish, too, out of my commission."

Mark waved his hand. "Forget it."

"The kittens are just minutes old. She'll be nursing them soon, and grooming them. Would it be all right to move her bed in here? She'll need somewhere clean to take the kittens when she's up to it. We'll put the bed back in her room later."

"Sure."

Ellie conjured up a shaky smile in gratitude. Her head started spinning, and she leaned against the door frame for support.

"I'll take care of moving the bed," he said gently. "You need some rest."

She allowed him to guide her in the direction of the guest room. He turned the covers back, an odd expression on his face. "Do you need anything?"

Her head ached too much to keep her eyes open. "Can you spare a T-shirt?" she asked. "I hadn't planned on staying over."

Mark returned in a few minutes with the shirt over his arm, but Ellie lay sound asleep on top of the covers, fully dressed. He shook his head, reaching forward to touch her smooth cheek, flushed from fever. As gently as possible, so as not to disturb her, Mark undressed her down to her panties. Stopping only long enough to caress the mouse tattoo just above her bikini line, he then pulled his baggy T-shirt over her tousled head. She murmured his name groggily, then turned on her side and curled into a sleeping ball. When the temptation to stay and cuddle her became overwhelming, Mark rose quickly and left, closing the door behind him.

After moving the cat's bed to the closet a few feet away from the birthing nest, Mark dialed Ellie's apartment and assured a wary Manny that both patients were resting. Then he climbed into his own bed as he'd meant to hours ago. But the sleep he craved eluded him. The vibes radiating from Ellie in the room down the hall beckoned him, and Mark couldn't remember ever having to exert so much control just to lie still.

11

"ELLIE." Mark was shaking her awake, gently calling her name from a distance. She moved forward through the fog until at last she managed to open her eyes. She blinked, trying to adjust to the daylight, and attempted to raise her head. A splitting pain shot through her ears, and she groaned, resting back against the pillow.

"Ellie," he repeated, his voice slightly muffled. "I think something's wrong with Esmerelda. Who is your vet?"

She licked her dry lips with her thick tongue. "Dr. Doolittle," she croaked.

"Here, have some ice." He held ice chips to her mouth and she took them with her tongue, the wetness pure heaven in her sandy mouth. "Ellie, I'm serious, I need the name of your veterinarian."

"Dr. Doolittle," she repeated. "Dr. Edmund Doolittle. His office is in Midtown. What's wrong?"

His green eyes were full of worry. "I'm not sure, but Esmerelda's acting funny. She's sneezing. Do you think she could be allergic to *me* all of a sudden?"

Smiling, Ellie shook her head painfully. She tried to sit up, but he pressed her back. "Wait until I call the vet, then I'll help you up." With a start, Ellie realized he'd tied a white handkerchief over his mouth and nose. No wonder he sounded so far away. She pointed, giggling weakly.

He shrugged. "Between the cold germs and cat hair, I figured I'd be safer this way. Someone has to take care of the rest of you." His statement seeped into her, drenching every dehydrated pore. Watching him dial directory assistance from the phone in her room, a myriad of feelings assaulted Ellie, ranging from euphoria that this was the way life was supposed to be, to sorrow that it wasn't reality.

Ever so slowly, so as not to trigger the bolting headache, Ellie inched her way up to a semireclining position on the pillow. After a series of transfers, Mark got through to the doctor. Still talking through the handkerchief, he explained the situation of Esmerelda being in his care, then described the cat's condition.

"The kittens are clean. Five of them. Esmerelda is sneezing and wheezing a lot, plus her nose and eyes are runny."

Ellie bit her bottom lip to keep from smiling at his concerned, serious tone. As if he were talking about a child.

"Yeah, she moved them to the clean bed. They've been trying to nurse, but I don't see any liquid coming out, and they're wearing her out, I think. Yeah, I put a bowl of water and some food next to the new bed, but she hasn't touched it."

After a minute, he covered the mouthpiece with his hand, still listening to the doctor. "He thinks she might have a respiratory infection. She won't be able to nurse for a while."

Alarm shot through Ellie. Would the kittens live?

Mark scribbled on a notepad. "Thanks, Doc. I'll let you know. Sure thing."

He hung up and turned to Ellie. "He says it's probably a virus and it'll have to run its course. Just in case, he says to refill the antibiotic she was taking for the bladder infection. And I'll need to pick up a bottle and a week's worth of formula for the kittens. I called my own doctor earlier for advice on what to do for you, so I'll go get everything we need and be back in a little while, okay?"

"I thought you went to law school, not med school," she whispered.

He leaned over as if to peck her on the cheek, then remembered the hankie and straightened abruptly, saying, "I won't be long. Try to get some rest."

But Ellie's eyelids were already floating down and Mark's voice fading away.

"OPEN WIDE, Esmerelda," Mark pleaded. The tablet had been easy enough to hide in her food before, but how could he get her to swallow it if she wasn't interested in eating? Following the vet's orders, he held her head with one hand, then tickled her chin to get her to open her mouth. Once he saw her pink tongue, he pushed the capsule into her mouth. "Ow!" he yelped when her teeth caught his skin as he pulled his finger out. Then he held the struggling cat's mouth shut until she swallowed. "Sorry about that, old girl," Mark mumbled through his mask. Then before he let her go, he wiped her eyes and nose with a clean handkerchief. "Now, let's see to your kittens."

He'd scrubbed his arms raw with antibacterial soap. Now he reached for the first tiny animal next to Esmerelda and cupped it in his large hand. He smiled. Its eyes were still tightly closed, its face and front paws snowy white, the rest of its sleek fur as orange as its mother's. "Boots," he dubbed it, not sure of the sex. "Open up, Boots." Mark moved the tiny nipple of the bottle to its lips. At first it resisted, but when he drizzled a few drops of the warm formula over the kitten's mouth, the seeking tongue licked it up, finally seeking the nipple. Astonishment struck Mark as the tiny animal nursed, its miniature paws kneading his hand. A strange paternal feeling crept over him. He held the kitten within Esmerelda's sight the entire time, but scant minutes passed before the tiny stomach filled and the suckling stopped.

He named the solid black one EightBall, the solid orange one, Juice, the black and white one, Jersey, and the white one with a splash of orange under its chin, BowTie. Each of them caught on as quickly as their first sibling, and were soon sleeping contentedly next to their mother. Mark even coaxed Esmerelda to take a few bites of her food, and to drink her fill of water. Then he removed the food as the vet suggested.

That done, he checked in on his other patient, pleased to see her rousing from her nap at the sound of the guest-room door opening. She was a mess, her hair limp and matted, her eyes still red and puffy. But she was beautiful. "Hey," he said, his voice filtering through the ever-present mask.

"How is she?" Ellie asked weakly.

"The doctor says she'll be fine. I got her to take the medicine, then fed the kittens."

Ellie smiled. "I wish I could've seen that."

"How are you feeling?"

"Like I've been run over by that beer truck of yours."

I'm starting to feel that way, too. "Are you hungry?"

She paused, as if checking with her stomach. "Yeah."

"Then let's get you up for a shower, and I'll fix you some soup."

"I kind of like being horizontal."

"But you'll feel so much better," he encouraged. "I'll get the water hot, then come back for you."

As he adjusted the spray of water, Mark had the distinct feeling he teetered on some kind of threshold: seeing an attractive woman in a near state of undress and not acting upon an urge. It struck him as very domestic, and not sexy at all. Perhaps this was what he needed to work through his lust for Ellie, to see her in an unsexy light.

"Are you ready?" he asked, walking into the room.

"I rather like it here," she insisted again, obviously not looking forward to the effort.

"Up you go," he said, placing a hand on her shoulder and easing her up slowly.

"Oh, my head," she said, grimacing.

"Sit on the edge of the bed for a moment to gather your strength," he instructed.

"You look ridiculous with that handkerchief tied over your mouth."

"You don't want to know how you look. Come on, try to stand up."

After a few false starts, Ellie made it to her feet, leaning heavily on Mark's arm for support. "I feel so weak," she moaned. "My teeth hurt."

Mark guided her into the guest bath toward the large shower stall. He'd set a stool beneath the spray so she wouldn't have to stand. The hot water had moistened the air, steam rising and swirling toward the ceiling.

"Oh, my God," Ellie said when she caught a glimpse of herself in the mirror. "Who is that?"

Mark chuckled and walked her to the shower door. "Here's your towel and some sweats. Do you need anything else?"

"While you're here, I might as well humiliate myself completely and ask you to help me with this shirt. I don't think I can lift my arms and pull at the same time."

Taking a deep breath, Mark nodded. She raised her arms slowly, then Mark slid the flimsy cotton shirt up her body and over her head. At the sight of her tan lines and skimpy undies, his body overheated immediately. *Unsexy. Yeah, right.*

"Thanks, sheik," she mumbled, obviously still amused by his makeshift mask. She rolled down her panties and kicked them off, then opened the shower door and collapsed onto the stool. Ellie leaned forward to let the warm water run over her head. "Come back in about an hour," she gurgled.

Mark exited gratefully.

BY VISUALIZING Mitzi Gaynor singing "I'm Gonna Wash That Man Right Outta My Hair," Ellie managed to give most of herself a once-over with the soapy sponge. Then she must have dozed off for a while, because she was jarred awake by a blast of cool water from the showerhead. "Mighty scrawny water heater for such a big house," she grumbled. Only the freezing air from the ceiling fan spurred her into putting forth enough effort to leave the shower and wrap the towel loosely around her chilling body. But within another few steps, she felt light-headed. Reaching for the wall, Ellie slid down to rest on the floor, leaning forward to put her head between her knees.

She heard the tap at the door, but her neck refused to raise her head. Taking a shallow breath, she mumbled a response into the towel cave she'd created for herself. Suddenly Mark was by her side, worry evident in his voice.

"Ellie, are you all right? I should have stayed."

"I'm fine," she said into the thick terry cloth. "Just light-headed."

"Light-headed? You're probably dehydrated." He tugged

on her arm to pull her body up a few inches, then swung her gently into his arms, and carried her.

Even through the haze of sickness, Ellie remembered when he'd last carried her to bed, it was to make love to her for the first time. That had happened last year sometime. Or was it yesterday? She couldn't be sure. She only knew she felt much better lying down on the fresh, cool sheets. Mark must have changed them. She opened her eyes and smiled at him. "You were right. The shower did make me feel better."

Mark pulled the wet towel from her body and helped her tug the covers up to her neck. Then he disappeared for a few minutes, returning with a tray of soup, crackers and two glasses of water. The smell alone revived her enough to sit up. And she was able to feed herself. She felt her strength returning a little with each bite. "I'm sorry, Mark, I should have stayed home. Now you'll probably be sick, too."

He smiled behind his hankie and pointed to it. "Besides," he added, "I had a flu shot in the spring."

"Is that what I've got?"

"My doctor said it sounded like the flu." He handed her two tablets. "For body aches," he said.

Got anything for heartaches? she wondered. "I want to see the kittens. Are they adorable?"

His cheekbones rose above the handkerchief and his eyes danced. "Yeah. Finish eating and then see how you feel."

"How's Esmerelda?"

"Relieved, I think, that the kittens are fed."

"She'll love you for it," Ellie said, quickly taking another spoonful of soup. When she glanced up, he was staring at her, his eyes unreadable. Suddenly her stomach rolled. "Oh, God." She brought her hand to her mouth.

"What?" Mark asked, his voice anxious.

"I'm going to throw up."

Mark jumped to his feet, searching for a container, then thrust a small trash can in front of her, not a second too soon. Between every retch, Ellie prayed a time warp would open and swallow her into another dimension. Could she be any more humiliated in front of this man?

Yes, she decided an hour later when her menstrual cramps began. Fortified with a smaller second helping of broth, Ellie dragged herself to the edge of the bed and stared in horror at her reflection in the mirror. Her hair had dried pasted to her head in the back, then straight up on end all around. "I look like the Statue of Liberty," she moaned, trying to smooth down the spikes. She struggled into the sweats Mark had laid at the foot of the bed, then stumbled into the bathroom to splash water on her blotchy face and comb her high hair.

"You're up," Mark said, his voice cheerful. He leaned against the door of the bedroom, but could see her standing through the open door of the bathroom.

"Yeah," said Ellie, embarrassment flooding her body. "And so is my hair."

He grinned. "Feeling better?"

"Uh, well, no, as a matter of fact, things have taken a turn for the worse. Is there a convenience store close by?"

"Just down a couple of blocks." He stepped into her room, concern in his eyes. What do you need?"

"Could you drive me?"

"No way you're getting out in your condition. Look at you."

"Thanks."

"I mean, look how sick you are. You're hanging on to the vanity to stand up, for Pete's sake. I'll get whatever you need."

"Okay. I need tampons."

He blinked. "T-tampons?"

Ellie raised her hands. "Forget it, I'll go."

"No," Mark said hurriedly. "That's all right, I'll be glad to." He started to leave, then turned back. "Anything else?" he asked, swallowing.

"While you're in that section, could you grab some panty shields?"

MARK SAT IN HIS CAR, scoping out the parking lot of the convenience store. He'd run into neighbors and colleagues here on more than one occasion. He closed his eyes and tried to remember which aisle held feminine-hygiene products. He'd bought painkillers once in the middle aisle and figured those two things should be pretty close. After all, it was all kind of...medical, wasn't it?

The object was to get in, get the goods and get out. If he waited until the cashier's line dwindled to one or two people, he figured he could buy what he needed and be safely back in his car within three minutes.

He watched two people pump gas and then walk in to pay for it. They were the only two customers in the store. He pulled a ball cap low over his forehead, and entered the store. He kept his eyes focused on the medicine aisle, but came face-to-face with a rack of picnic supplies. He glanced over at the beer case and saw milk instead. They'd rearranged the entire store.

A woman in a striped smock was sweeping up a spill a few feet away. "Can I help you?"

"Yeah," Mark said. "Can you show me to the aspirin?"

"Follow me, sir."

She walked slowly to aisle two and swept her arm at the array of painkillers as Mark scanned the shelves for the items he'd really come to purchase.

"We have regular, extra strength, buffered, childproof caps, nighttime—"

"Buffered will be fine," he said, then took the bottle she gave him.

The clerk stood with her hands on the broom, looking at him. "Anything else, sir?"

"Uh, I'll just look around."

"Go right ahead." She turned and shuffled toward the front of the store.

Mark walked up and down each of the eight aisles, keeping his eyes peeled for anything that said Personal or Feminine. Nothing. He made a second pass, this time more slowly. Nada.

He glanced around nervously and spotted the same clerk watching him closely, this time from behind a counter. She elbowed the cashier, a sour-looking teenager, and whispered something, nodding toward him. The cashier carefully pushe a button on her console, her eyes glued on him.

Mark grunted in frustration. *They think I'm stealing some thing.*

Within a few seconds, a jacketed, severe-looking olde woman appeared. Her badge said Store Manager. *Great.*

"Can I help you, sir?"

"Uh, yeah," he said, keeping his voice low. "My...wi sent me out to pick up some personal things."

The woman frowned in confusion. "Personal things?"

"You know," he said, making vague gestures with hi hands. "Woman stuff."

"Woman stuff?"

He sighed. "You know, *pads* and stuff."

"You're looking for menstruation products?"

He smiled tightly and nodded, admitting defeat.

"Right this way." She took him to an end cap in the fron of the store which held a mind-boggling array of colored packages.

"Did you need pads or tampons?" she asked, her face serious, her voice rigid.

"Uh, tampons."

"Will that be deodorant or nondeodorant?"

"The pink box will be fine," Mark mumbled, heat rushin to his face.

"Slim, regular, plus or super-duper?"

"She's snug—I mean, small...she's a small lady." H reached up to rub his hand across his mouth.

"That has no relevance in this case, sir."

"Uh...regular, I guess."

She sighed. "Twelve count or twenty-four?"

"I'm not sure." Mark looked around, then leaned forwar and whispered, "And I'm supposed to get some panty things too."

"Panty shields?" she asked loudly. The clerks giggle openly, as did a few onlookers.

"Yeah," he murmured.

"Regular or winged?"

Mark sighed, pinching the bridge of his nose with forefinger and thumb. "Just give me two of everything."

She stacked his arms full, and carried a couple of packages toward the counter, herself. Except now the cashier's line had grown to about a dozen. Mark swore under his breath and inched his way forward, careful of his cumbersome load.

He maneuvered around a beer display, but his knee accidently nudged the mountain of twelve-pack bottles. The seemingly unending sound of crashing bottles was superseded only by the security alarm triggered from the shattering glass.

By the time the cops arrived, the clerks had most of the mess cleaned up and tallied.

Mark used his credit card to pay for two hundred thirty-eight dollars and fifty-nine cents' worth of "woman stuff" and beer.

"BLACKWELL!"

Mark jarred awake, his eyes flying open, his head jerking back. The men around the table chuckled as Mark shook his head to clear it, then repositioned himself in the conference-room chair. He'd fallen asleep in the middle of a staff meeting!

Ray Ivan frowned. "Are we keeping you up, son?"

"No, sir, sorry." Mark ground his teeth in frustration. Between frequent kitten feedings and Ellie's bouts of vomiting, he wasn't getting much rest. Two sleepless nights in a row had taken their toll.

When the meeting ended, Specklemeyer said, "Keeping late nights, Blackwell? I wonder what you could possibly be doing." He flashed a knowing smile, then trotted out when Mark's hands tightened on the chair arms.

Patrick walked out with him. "Why don't you take the afternoon off, Mark? You look beat."

"Ellie's got the flu," Mark explained, rubbing his eyes. "And the kids—I mean, the kittens...never mind. That's a very good idea. I'll see you tomorrow."

On the drive home, Mark berated himself over the predicament he'd gotten himself into. In just two days, he'd had his fill of domesticity. He breathed a quick prayer of thanks he'd broken it off with Ellie before all this mess. At least she' been feeling better this morning, so he'd be rid of her and he cats soon. No more sneezing, no more litter boxes, no mor heating pads. Good riddance! He'd probably have to take nap in his car when he got home, just to have some peace an quiet.

Mark wheeled into the driveway and pulled into the garage already dreading the melee that awaited him inside. He sighec pushing open the kitchen door, waiting for the scents of ca milk and chicken soup to hit him. His nose wrinkled. Disin fectant?

"Ellie?" he called, walking through the kitchen. A note o the counter stopped him. Ellie's feminine writing curled acros the page.

> Great news! We have a new landlord who lifted the no-pet rule. Manny and a friend came over to pick us up today and take us home. I took the painting, too. It's not much, but I did a little cleaning to help repay you for all the trouble. We can't thank you enough. Ellie and Esmerelda.

A paw print in—lipstick?—stood out by Esmerelda's name The extra key lay nearby.

Mark stood stock-still. Not even a goodbye? Who's to know she wouldn't have a relapse once she got home? And sh didn't know the kittens' feeding schedule the way he did. O that BowTie ate better when his little ears were rubbed. Th kittens' eyes weren't even open yet, for heaven's sake! Wha was she thinking?

Wadding the note into a ball, he stomped upstairs. Not sign of them anywhere. Every room sparkled, smelling clea and fresh. Not a cat hair in sight.

Mark sneezed.

"SAY CHEESE," Ellie said to the furry group squirming on th love seat. She snapped several pictures.

"What are you doing now?" Manny asked, walking into the living room.

"Just finishing up a roll of film. I thought I'd send out birth announcements for Esmerelda."

"I think your fever must have risen higher than anyone realized."

"Oh, stop. It'll be fun," Ellie insisted. "And a great way to find homes for the kittens. I'll send them to everyone we know."

Manny stooped to catch a wriggling kitten before it rolled off the cushion. "How soon can they be weaned?"

"Well, they're not quite two weeks old yet, so maybe another four weeks, possibly five since Esmerelda only started nursing yesterday."

"Have you heard from Papa Blackwell?"

Ellie's heart stirred. "No," she said brightly. "Why?"

"I was hoping I'd underestimated him. Unfortunately, it seems I was right again."

"He did take good care of us," Ellie said, practically to herself. The way he'd watched over them in his home did more to tangle her heartstrings than his previous wild lovemaking. While he'd held the trash can for her to empty her stomach, she'd felt herself sinking deeper in love with Mark. At that point, she'd vowed to leave as soon as she was physically able. That she'd been able to take the cats with her had been a bonus.

"I suppose you'll see him when you deliver the portrait."

Ellie glanced over at the twin portraits leaning against the wall, waiting to be framed. "I was thinking of having it couriered over when it's ready."

"Why don't you get dolled up and deliver it in person?"

"Manny, do you honestly think a cute outfit is going to erase the memory of him seeing my partially digested food?"

"Okay, I see your point. What are you going to do with the nude?" he asked, his voice wistful.

"Hmm." Ellie frowned. "I'm not sure. Harry will give me a better deal on the framing if I have them done at the same time. Afterward, maybe I can alter the face enough to sell it."

"You're welcome to use mine."

She grinned. "I might take you up on that."

When Ellie rewound the film and put away her camera, sh discovered the two undeveloped rolls from the Blackwell pic nic. Adding them to her backpack, she then changed into rid ing togs and grabbed her helmet.

"Back in a few minutes," she yelled.

It was a beautiful day for a ride, and Ellie hadn't been ou much since recovering from her bout of the flu. She'd avoide it since she tended to think too much while cycling. And sh hadn't been ready to face the sad thoughts until now.

She loved him. With all her heart. She'd seen glimpses o the kind of partner he would be. They could have made thing work.

If only he loved her, too.

Mark Blackwell might have been fooled by the pheromone in the beginning, but now that he'd seen her at her worst an without the influence of the love chemicals, she didn't have chance of moving his heart the way he'd shaken hers. So she' grieve for a few months, then pick up the pieces and sta looking again. Maybe she'd give Steve Willis a call.

Ellie dropped off the film at a one-hour developing cente then went in search of dried fruits and herbs for her lates perfume brainstorm. One good thing about being finished wit the pheromones, she could wear her customized fragrance once again.

But, she decided as she rode by the sexy traffic cop withou garnering so much as a second glance, it was the *only* goo thing about not taking the pills. Her sex appeal had apparentl nose-dived to its normal basement level.

She took a few moments to study the photos when sh picked them up. She ordered lots of reprints of the best grou picture of Esmerelda and the kittens. The photos of the picni resurrected bittersweet memories. She'd gotten several goo candid shots, especially one picture of Mark with his ar around his mother. Gloria was smiling, looking flushed an pretty.

A thought struck Ellie, and she checked her watch, gaugin

the distance to Gloria's house. Just far enough for a good ride, she decided, and she'd be back in time to pick up the reprints.

Ellie pumped her legs furiously, enjoying the rush of adrenaline. After several blocks, apartment buildings and commercial property gave way to small older homes, with tiny picturesque yards. She slowed her pedaling to check the street signs, then turned down the road where Gloria Blackwell lived.

Wheeling into the neat driveway, she hopped off her bike and walked it to the sidewalk. After removing her helmet and running her hand through her hair, she took a deep breath, then removed the photos from her pack.

She climbed the steps leading to the pretty white clapboard home, nervousness rattling in her chest. After ringing the bell and waiting a few minutes, Ellie was tempted to leave the package of photos against the door and go, but suddenly the door opened and Gloria stood there, her hair rolled in large lavender curlers.

"Yes?" she said cautiously, her hand going to her hair.

"Hi, Mrs. Blackwell. I'm Ellie Sutherland. We met—"

Recognition dawned on the woman's face. "At the picnic, I remember," she said tartly.

"Yes, well...I brought you the pictures I snapped that afternoon." She extended the envelope to Mark's mother. "There is one of you and Mark I think you'll be especially pleased with."

"Why, thank you," Gloria said quietly. "But why didn't you just give the pictures to Mark?"

Ellie's heart lurched. "We're not seeing each other anymore."

Gloria's eyes brightened a fraction. "Oh?" She flipped through the photos, a small smile playing across her mouth. "My, Audra looks hippy in that flowered dress."

"Well, I guess I'll be going." Ellie started to turn away.

"Would you like to come in?" Gloria asked, obviously uncomfortable but mindful of her manners.

Ellie smiled and shook her head. "Thank you, but I really must be going. I have some other photos to pick up—" She stopped as an idea struck her. "Mrs. Blackwell, do you share Mark's allergies?"

Gloria smiled. "Me? Heavens, no. His father was always the sniffly one. My son inherited it from him, I suppose." She counted on her fingers. "Marcus is allergic to grass, pollen, animals, feathers—"

"Whipped cream," Ellie added without thinking. When Gloria frowned in confusion, Ellie said weakly, "The foamy kind." Then she cleared her throat noisily. "Well, anyway, maybe I will come in for just a moment." She flashed her most persuasive smile. "Do you have any pets?"

"OH," Monica cooed. "Aren't they adorable?"

"Um," Mark murmured, studying the birth announcement Monica had received. The question "Do you have a home for one of my babies?" was lettered in bold print across the bottom of the card holding the photo. Written as a letter from Esmerelda, the announcement doubled as a solicitation to adopt one of her precious infants. The kittens' eyes were open, their heads and paws woefully out of proportion to their tiny bodies. He noted with relief that BowTie, the runt of the litter, seemed to be holding his own with his rowdy siblings.

"I think I'll take one," Monica said. "Would you tell Ellie the next time you see her?"

Mark cleared his throat. "We, uh, aren't seeing each other anymore." He shuffled through a handful of phone messages she'd handed him a few minutes earlier, hoping one of them would be from Ellie.

"What? But you were engaged!"

Mark frowned at her wide-eyed expression. "Well, now we're not."

"Just like that?"

Irritation shot through him. "No, not just like that. We both agreed we weren't right for each other."

Monica shook her head in disbelief. "Are you blind? You're perfect for each other."

Mark raised his hands in astonishment. "We're complete opposites!"

"Like I said, the perfect match."

Shaking his head, Mark headed toward his office. "You're not making sense."

"Well, at least I know why you've been so testy the last few days," she called after him.

"I have *not* been testy the last few days!" Mark yelled as he slammed his door.

12

MARK SPENT a restless Sunday morning doing nothing of significance. It was shaping up to be a blah, overcast day, and he had a mood to match. He sat down heavily on the couch and began flipping through channels. A lump under his hip caught his attention, and he pulled out a toy cloth mouse. One of Esmerelda's less destructive pastimes. The pink mouse resembled Ellie's tattoo, the memory of which had him shifting positions again.

Why couldn't he get the woman out of his mind? Somehow she'd wormed her way into his heart, then sprouted barbs, at once anchoring her image and promising bloodshed if he tried to dislodge it.

He reached over to pick up the cordless phone and dialed his mother's number, thinking he'd probably regret this phone call later. "Hi, Mom," he said.

"Hello, dear, it's so nice to hear from you. Where have you been keeping yourself the last few days?"

He swung Esmerelda's mouse by the tail. "Mostly at the office, you know, working late."

"You're so industrious, Marcus, I suppose you get it from my side of the family." She sighed. "Lord knows, your father never hit a lick at anything, God love him."

Mark frowned and leaned forward to place his elbows on his knees. "Mom, I've never asked you this before, but you and Dad seemed so different, why did you marry him? I'm sure you could have found a better provider."

She was silent for a long moment.

"Mom?"

"I'm here," she whispered.

"I didn't mean to upset you."

"If I'm upset with anyone, it's myself. I guess it's easy to point out a person's shortcomings. To other people, I suppose your father and I seemed somewhat the odd couple. I'm sorry I never took the time to tell you why I fell in love with Rudy."

He sat in silence, afraid to interrupt her train of thought.

"Your father was a wonderful, caring man, Marcus. His heart was ten times bigger than his bank account, and I knew that when he proposed." She laughed softly. "I was a comely woman in my day, and I had a fair amount of suitors, some of them real catches. But not one of them could make me laugh like Rudy."

His mother cleared her throat. "I followed my heart instead of my head. And you know what? I might have wished for your father to be more financially stable, but I never regretted my decision to be his wife."

Mark's eyes clouded and his insides tingled. Ellie's face floated in and out of his mind, taunting him. *Follow your heart, follow your heart…*

"Well, enough about that," Gloria said brightly. "How's the little painter?"

It took a few seconds for Mark to recover from his surprise. "You mean Ellie?"

"Yes, Ellie. She came by the house the other day, you know."

He frowned. "No, I didn't know."

"Brought me pictures she'd taken at the picnic—she got a lovely one of you and me together."

"That's nice." Was that cheeriness in his mother's voice?

"She offered me a kitten, too. She said you'd helped nurse them when the mother couldn't. And got her through a bout with the flu, I hear." Her voice rolled with innuendo. "Is there something you're not telling me, son?"

"What do you mean?"

"You like this girl, don't you?"

"Well, sure I like her—"

"Do you love her?"

Mark snorted. "What kind of question is that?"

"A legitimate one considering you bottle-fed five kittens for her."

She had a point. "I haven't made up my mind how I feel about her."

Gloria clucked. "It's none of my business, but I wouldn't dawdle if I were you."

"What did you two talk about?"

"Lots of things—she's really very nice, Marcus, even if she is a bit quirky. She found me a fourth for Sunday bridge tomorrow."

"She plays bridge?"

"No, but she knew that Ray Ivan plays and she called him right up."

"My partner is playing bridge with you tomorrow?"

"Stella is making coffee cake and we thought we might splurge on a bottle of sherry."

Mark smiled and shook his head. "Sounds like a day."

"Oh, look at the time," she exclaimed. "I have an appointment to get my hair done."

He laughed and injected suggestion into his voice. "Go, Mom."

"Oh, you." She giggled, clearly pleased at the prospect of having a beau.

"Uh, Mom, I was wondering…did Ellie have anything to say about, well, you know…me and her?"

"Hmm." He could picture her squinting at the ceiling. "I recall her saying something about…" She paused.

"Yeah?" he prompted.

"No," she said suddenly, "come to think of it, I don't think she said a word about the two of you."

"Oh," he said, frowning. Disappointment squeezed his heart.

"I'll call you tomorrow when I get back from bridge," his mother promised. "Bye now."

Mark hung up the phone, then stood and grabbed his keys, fully planning to drive to the office for a few hours. Instead, he drove around in circles before he finally parked at the train station and caught the line speeding toward Underground Atlanta. Maybe she would be there, drawing caricatures. And what if she is? his conscience probed. I'll think of something brilliant to say, he promised himself.

Underground Atlanta, located in the center of downtown, boasted nearly a hundred shops in its restored multilevel structure. The lower level, abandoned early in the century when the entire city was elevated, now resembled a town street, with shops on either side, the ceiling stretching far above the foot traffic. The quaint atmosphere and curbside entertainers combined to make it a favorite place for locals and tourists.

Mark strolled the length of the cobbled main street, moving with the crowd, stopping to watch a humorous puppeteer, tossing a dollar into the man's hat at the conclusion of the show. The small knot of people gathered at the end of the indoor street might have gone unnoticed by him, except for the glimpse of a floppy hat. He walked closer, carefully staying out of Ellie's line of vision. His heart pounded at the sight of her smile as she invited a young woman to pose for a caricature. Stepping close enough to watch her sketch, Mark marveled once again over her talent, and her ability to banter with the audience as she drew.

She must have inquired into the woman's hobbies because the finished drawing showed the woman holding a flute. The woman thanked her and paid for her drawing, then Ellie glanced around for another customer. Suddenly her eyes landed on Mark, and she stopped in obvious surprise. He tingled in response to her expression. He'd been too rash in suggesting they stop seeing each other. Perhaps she would go to dinner with him this evening.

"Sir," she called to him, "would you like to have your picture drawn?"

The crowd turned for his response, and he nodded, happily stepping up and taking a seat in front of her.

She frowned, studying him in an exaggerated fashion before beginning the sketch. Mark remembered the queen-bee drawing of his mother and wondered how Ellie would portray him.

"Tell me about yourself," she said, obviously for the crowd's sake.

"I'm an attorney," he said simply.

She smiled, and spoke to the crowd. "Shall I draw him as a shark?" The audience tittered.

He shrugged good-naturedly. Ellie picked up a pastel crayon and began drawing on her sketch pad. Mark couldn't see the picture from where he sat. She looked beautiful in a pink denim jacket buttoned up to her chin over a long flowered skirt. She was multifaceted: Ellie the artist, Ellie the perfume maker, Ellie the wild lover. He smiled. And all of her personas made him happy, made him laugh. *"But not one of them could make me laugh like Rudy..."*

As she sketched, she asked him questions she already knew the answers to.

"Are you a visitor?"

Mark played along. "No, a native."

"Are you married?"

"Single."

"Do you like cats?"

"I'm allergic."

The audience watched, their faces splitting into grins as Mark's drawing progressed. He squirmed. Would she put him in his sports car? A briefcase in one hand and a phone in the other? A fancy suit and harried expression? He wouldn't blame her if she did. Work had always been his top priority. Could it be his values were beginning to shift toward settling down? Mark felt an odd sensation settle in his stomach. What good were all his possessions if he had no one to share them with? And not just anyone. He wanted Ellie.

"There," Ellie exclaimed, finishing with a flourish. The crowd laughed outright when she shifted the easel toward him for his reaction. Mark swallowed, then smiled. She'd drawn him standing, a white handkerchief tied around his mouth, concentrating intently, a squirming kitten in one hand, a bottle in the other. Four other kittens climbed his jeans legs.

"It's great," he said, looking into Ellie's bright eyes. "How are they?"

"The kittens? I still haven't found homes for Jersey, EightBall or BowTie, but I'm hopeful."

"Mom said you'd talked her into adopting one. By the way, thanks for taking her the pictures."

Ellie shrugged and nodded. "No problem."

"And for arranging the bridge matchup."

Another shrug. "I owed your mother one—and Ray, too."

He fished around for any scrap of conversation. "Monica said she'd take a kitten."

"Great," she said, her smile jarring his heart. "Three down and two to go."

Listen to your heart...do you love her?...don't dawdle... "Ellie—"

"Hey," a fair-haired man exclaimed, walking up to Ellie. "How much longer?"

"This was my last drawing, Steve," Ellie said, smiling up at the man. Her face flushed a becoming rose at his appearance—she was obviously pleased to see him.

Mark's gut twisted at the man's familiarity with Ellie. She tore his drawing off her pad and handed it to him. Instantly, Mark reached for his wallet.

Ellie stopped him, holding up a hand. "It's on the house." She stood and turned to the crowd. "Thank you, everyone, I'll be back next Sunday."

The Steve guy began to gather up her supplies, and Mark stood awkwardly. Ellie folded her easel, then glanced at him with a half smile. "See you around," she said, lifting her hand in a friendly wave, then walked off with the man's hand at her elbow.

Mark stood like a statue, his eyes riveted on the couple. At the end of the indoor street, Ellie stopped in front of a bag lady who sat sprawled on the curb, her possessions huddled around her. He saw Ellie reach into her purse and extract a couple of bills, then hand them to the woman, smiling and saying a few words before she went on her way.

Ellie, already on a tight budget, giving away her hard-earned money to a needy person. *Just like Dad...Rudy would have been crazy about Ellie.* He watched helplessly as the blond man put his arm around her shoulder and kissed her hair.

Mark wondered if he'd caught a lingering flu bug, after all. He suddenly felt very sick to his stomach.

"THE PAINTINGS turned out great," Harry said, emerging from the back of the framing shop with one in each arm.

Desire washed over Ellie as Mark's face leaped from one picture, his body from the other. An ornate cherry-wood frame lent more formality to his business portrait, a simple black wood frame set off the nude perfectly.

"Great," she agreed with a forced smile. "I'll take the nude with me. Courier the bust to this address and add it to my bill." She handed the framer a slip of paper.

"Wait and I'll wrap them both," he said, winking. "Else you might have a trail of women following you home wanting this guy's number."

In the few minutes Ellie waited, she changed her mind a dozen times about having the painting delivered. Maybe she should take it herself, to gauge Mark's reaction to her. He'd come to Underground a few days ago, presumably to see her, although she couldn't be sure. Maybe he did care for her, after all. But without the pheromones, how long could she keep his interest? And she couldn't bear going through another breakup.

Harry appeared with the wrapped nude a few minutes later. "My driver was leaving with a delivery, so I gave him the bust. It's already on its way."

Ellie nodded. It was for the best.

But on the walk home, doubts nagged at Ellie. She'd never felt toward any man what she felt with Mark. Steve Willis was a nice man, but no feelings surfaced when he kissed her. What if Mark Blackwell was the one great love of her life, and she let him slip through her fingers because he reminded her of her father? Mark wasn't Joe Sutherland. In his early years, her dad would never have nursed kittens and gone shopping for feminine-hygiene articles.

Ellie took a deep breath and turned in the direction of the clinic. After a few minutes' walk, she pushed open the door and asked a receptionist to page Freda. Soon, Freda emerged, her face folding with puzzlement when she saw Ellie.

"What brings you here?" the woman asked.

"Kittens," Ellie said, extending one of Esmerelda's birth announcements. "I'm trying to find homes for them and wondered if you'd be interested."

It was the first genuinely happy smile she'd seen on the woman's face. "My tabby passed on two months ago. I've been meaning to go to the shelter to find another, but I couldn't bring myself to replace her just yet."

"The black female is still unspoken for."

Freda nodded, satisfied. "I'll take her."

"Great," Ellie said, smiling. Then she glanced side to side, shifting slightly. "Uh, Freda, can we talk?"

The gray-haired woman checked the watch on her wrist. "I've got about ten minutes, come on back."

Ellie chewed her bottom lip nervously, wondering how the woman would react to her request.

"I've been wondering about you and your fellow," Freda said, glancing over her shoulder at Ellie as they entered her small office. "How did you make out?"

Ellie shut the door. "That's what I wanted to talk to you about."

Freda's eyebrows went up. "Oh?"

"I need more pills."

After a few seconds of hesitation, Freda replied, "I can't do that."

"Please?" Ellie pleaded, folding her hands together. Tears welled and spilled over her cheeks. "I've never been so miserable in my life. I love him."

Freda shook her head. "It's impossible—"

"I'll pay you," Ellie said through her tears. "Whatever it takes, just a few weeks' supply, just long enough to regain his attention and show him how really good we can be together."

"The pills are controlled, I can't distribute them outside the study."

Ellie sniffled loudly. "Then put me back in the study."

Handing her a tissue, Freda said, "You've already been

through one cycle of pills, you wouldn't be a pure study subject again so soon."

"You've got to help me." Ellie sobbed. "What am I going to do?" She blew her nose noisily, beseeching Freda.

The lab-coated woman sat back in her chair and sighed, then rose and crossed to a file cabinet. Opening the drawer, she fingered through several folders, finally stopping to extract one. Ellie saw her name on it. She hiccuped.

Freda studied the file, flipping through several pages quickly, obviously looking for a particular piece of information. At last she found it, because understanding dawned on her face. "Just what I suspected," she muttered thoughtfully.

Ellie held her breath. When she could wait no longer, she asked, "Can you help me?"

Lifting her head to study Ellie, Freda's eyes narrowed. "What I'm about to tell you could cost me my job, so you have to swear to keep this quiet."

Her heart pounded. "What is it?" Ellie asked, her tears now dry from fear.

"Promise?" Freda asked.

"I promise," Ellie agreed, crossing her heart solemnly.

Her new friend took a deep breath, then exhaled it roughly. "In the pheromones study we conducted..."

"Yes?" Ellie prompted, making a rolling motion with her hand. "What?"

"You were in the placebo group."

Confusion washed over her. "The placebo group?"

"That's right—you were taking sugar tablets. Any so-called effects of the pills you took were self-induced."

Ellie's arms and shoulders grew weak. She lifted her wobbly hands in question. "How can that be? Men kept smelling something."

"Maybe the extra sugar you were ingesting, maybe your natural scent—who knows? The power of suggestion is not to be underestimated." Freda sat back in her chair and crossed her arms. "Tell a woman she has the ability to attract any man she wants and watch her throw her shoulders back and begin to exude self-confidence." She leaned forward, waving a hand at Ellie. "Look at you—you have all the tools, you're pretty and funny and nice. What makes you think you need some silly old pills to make this man fall in love with you? If he's that blind, honey, then he can't be the one for you."

Ellie walked home, fighting back tears. Despite Freda's pep talk, her heart dragged heavily in the wake of the woman's revelation. If Mark had never been under the influence of pheromones, then he *had* been physically attracted to her, at least in the beginning. But it also meant whatever feelings he'd developed had waned naturally, and not because she'd suddenly run out of pills.

She'd been trying to make a mountain of commitment out of a molehill of lust.

The many tiny balls of fur that came running for her when she stepped into the apartment lifted her spirits somewhat. She grabbed a cold cola from the fridge and one for Manny as he came sauntering through the hall.

"Hey, girl."

"Hey."

He wrinkled his nose. "Are you going to be in a blue funk over Mark Blackwell forever?"

"Maybe," she said defiantly, cracking open the soda can and lifting it to her mouth.

He did the same. "Well, I for one get a boost every time I think about him getting caught in the bathroom at that restaurant." He laughed. "You've got to admit it's hilarious, El."

She smiled, begrudgingly lifted from her bad mood. "He could still get in worlds of trouble if Tony Specklemeyer decides to make an issue of it."

Manny stopped. "Is that the guy's name? Specklemeyer... Why does that name sound familiar?" He walked around the kitchen absently. "I can't think...wait a minute!" He snapped his fingers. "Does he drive a black Jaguar?"

Ellie shrugged. "Beats me. I do remember Mark saying he had a vanity license plate that says—"

"'HUNGRY,' in capital letters," Manny finished.

"How did you know that?"

He leaned against the counter, a cunning smile warming his

face. "Because that vile man circles the club where I work every other night, trying to pick up the performers as they leave." Manny shuddered. "He says the most disgusting things."

Ellie's mouth dropped open. "You're kidding?"

"Nope."

"Well, that's no crime."

"No," Manny agreed, "but you'd think the pot wouldn't be so anxious to call the kettle black if he could be thrown into the same dishwater."

She grinned. "You're right. I'll call Mark later and let him in on the news. I'll bet if he just drops a hint to this guy, he'll back off."

"If Mark hadn't been stupid enough to let you go, he wouldn't have to worry about any silly old rumors."

Ellie walked over and gave him a bear hug. "You're so good for me."

He pulled back in sudden recollection. "El, I forgot to tell you—you got a letter back from the perfume-making contest." He flipped through the mail on the counter and handed her an envelope.

Ripping it open, she scanned the letterhead, and read out loud. "Dear Ms. Sutherland, we are pleased to announce your formula, Irresistible You, has been chosen the winner—" Ellie screamed, then grabbed Manny and jumped up and down. "I won, I won, I won!" After a few moments of elation in which she kissed him and every cat within arm's reach, she continued reading. "Please contact us as soon as possible to arrange to collect your winnings, and to discuss your ideas for an entire product line. We look forward to hearing from you." She threw back her head and squealed in delight, dancing around the kitchen. In her exuberance, she knocked against the painting, the resulting tear in the wrapping paper exposing a glimpse of dark cherry wood.

Cherry? A tiny seed of dread sprouted in her stomach, then mushroomed when she ripped the paper farther and stared at Mark's business portrait.

"Oh, my God," she breathed. "Harry delivered the nude

to Mark's office by mistake!" Her eyes locked with Manny's. Thirty seconds later she pounded down the stairs, carrying the portrait under her arm. Running into the street, she hailed the first taxi she saw with a loud, ear-piercing whistle.

13

MONICA TAPPED on the door, then opened it a few inche "Mark," she said, holding up a letter and a bulky packag "Two things—Habitat for Humanity sent a thank-you lett for your donation, and a work schedule for the next hom being built."

He reached for it. "Thanks."

"If I may say so," she began tentatively.

"Yes?"

"Your donation was very generous, Mark. And for you t volunteer to help build a home for a needy family, well, it' a side of you I didn't know, but one I'm very impressed with.' She smiled and sincerity shone in her eyes.

"Thank you," he said softly, placing the letter on his desk

She held the large package toward him. "And your portra just arrived."

His pulse leaped. Ellie was here! Mark craned his neck t look around Monica. "Where is she?"

"Who?" Monica asked, confused.

"Ellie."

"I don't know. A courier delivered the painting."

"Oh." Mark tried to keep the dejection out of his voice but he knew he failed miserably. "Leave it, please."

Monica leaned it against his desk and made a hasty exi Mark turned back to the work spread across his desk an forced himself to concentrate. After a few minutes, he gav up, tossed the pen straight up in the air, then watched it bounc off a corner of his desk, disappearing over the edge.

He turned to look at the package. Even after all that work she didn't want to hand-deliver it. She didn't want to see him

Not that he blamed her. He'd made it coldly clear on the phone when he returned from Chicago that he didn't want to see her anymore. What an ass he'd been. Mark slammed his fist on his desk, but it only brought Monica back to the door.

"Mark? Are you okay?" she asked, concern written on her face.

"Fine," he said through clenched teeth. When she retreated, he massaged his throbbing hand, then reached for the painting. He fingered the wrapping for several seconds as sadness welled in him. He didn't want to see the portrait right now. He didn't want another painful reminder of Ellie and his foolish behavior.

He pushed a button on his phone. "Monica, please have maintenance come to pick up the painting and hang it." Within minutes, she entered his office again and retrieved the picture. Then Mark heard her give explicit directions to the man as to where it was to be hung.

Walking the length of his office, Mark rubbed his temples. He wished a headache would erupt, because then he'd at least have a reason for feeling lousy. This gnawing in his stomach and this heaviness in his chest were becoming unbearable. Damn! He never thought he'd let a woman get to him. Maybe he needed a vacation. That's it, he decided. *I'll go to some paradise for a couple of weeks and get Ellie out of my system. After all, she's just a woman.*

The Piedmont Park painting beckoned to him and he smiled. The picture never failed to lift his spirits. He walked over to it and absorbed the artist's impression of a day in the sun and wind. The colors, the movement, everything about it made him feel the way he did when his father took him to the park as a child. He could almost feel the grass between his toes and see his dad doing card tricks for a crowd of kids. They'd eat a cheese-sandwich picnic and fly kites, then roll up their pants and wade in the kiddie-pool. Back then, the days seemed to last forever, and every hour brought new and wonderful pleasures. He'd loved his father fiercely. He loved him still.

I really should contact the artist someday and tell him how much I enjoy this painting. He'd never before thought about the artist, and for the first time, his eyes searched the bottom right corner for a name. There it was, in white, but very smal and not quite clear. "E. Sutherland," he muttered slowly, the froze. Could it be? He double-checked the signature. A dir memory surfaced of the first day she'd walked into his office Nice picture, she'd said.

"Ellie," he murmured. A wondrous feeling began in hi chest and slowly radiated to his extremities. "I might hav known it was yours." Then he threw back his head an laughed. She had brought joy into his life even before he' known her. Mark laughed until he had to lean against the wal for support.

Another knock sounded, and Monica stuck her head in war ily. "Mark? Are you okay? I'm worried about you."

But Mark just grinned and chuckled, waving away her con cern. "Never better, Monica." She exited with a reluctant ex pression, then Mark slid down the wall to sit on the floor a he dissolved in laughter once again. When he'd finally re gained control, he shook his head at his own stupidity. H loved Ellie, he had from the beginning. But would she giv him another chance?

"I'm not letting her go without a fight," he said, pulling himself to his feet and crossing to his desk. He hadn't felt this good in days. Mark punched in Ellie's number and waited nervously to hear her voice.

"Hi, this is Ellie and Manny's place. You know the drill." Then a beep sounded.

He frowned, but began to speak. "Ellie, it's Mark. If you're there, please pick up, I need to talk to you right away." He hesitated a few seconds then said, "I l-l-lo—" He stuttered over the words, then tried again. "I l-l-lo—" Darnit, it was harder to say than he'd imagined. Mark took a deep breath. "I l-l-love you, Ellie. Please call me." He hung up slowly.

"I love you, too," Ellie said.

Mark spun around and his heart vaulted at the sight of her standing in his doorway with a package, a beaming Monica pushing her inside, closing the door.

Ellie swallowed tears that welled in her throat. He did love her.

He leaped to his feet and rushed toward her. Ellie leaned the wrapped painting against the wall, then met his embrace. He kissed her, lifting her off the ground and spinning her around. "Where did you come from?" he asked, grinning.

"Iowa," Ellie said, laughing through her tears.

"You were born in Iowa?"

Ellie nodded. "We have a lot of catching up to do."

Mark reached behind her to lock the door, then stepped to his desk and cleared the top with one sweep of his arm. He grinned. "We can start right here." Papers swirled to the ground at their feet.

Ellie's heart swelled as she allowed him to pull her to his desk. How she loved this man.

He lowered his head to hers and drew her into a deep kiss, his hands cupping her rear, pulling her against his arousal. They grabbed at each other's clothing, Ellie's skirt ending up around her waist, her panties on the ceiling fan. Mark's pants sagged around his ankles. Buttons from his shirt missiled against the wall as she yanked the front open.

"I don't have any protection," he whispered.

"I'd like to start a family as soon as possible," she replied throatily, positioning herself for his entry.

"Lots of kids?" he asked, sounding pleased.

"Five or so."

He plunged into her and Ellie stiffened with overwhelming desire.

"I feel like I could plant at least that many right now," he warned, moving inside her. They rocked together for a few seconds, then Ellie felt her ecstasy ballooning. "Mark," she whispered urgently. "Oh, Mark." He covered her mouth with his to absorb her scream of release. She heard, rather than felt, his shirt rip as she clawed his back. Suddenly he tensed and moaned low into her mouth, his body jerking in relief.

"I've missed you," he breathed.

After a few seconds, her pulse slowed. "I missed you, and so has Esmerelda."

Mark's eyes rolled heavenward. "I guess this means I'll have to paint my bedroom blue if we're ever going to have any privacy."

A loud commotion outside caught their attention. Mark frowned, pulled away, and started righting his clothes. "What's going on? It sounds like it's coming from down the hall."

Beads of perspiration popped out on Ellie's upper lip. "Mark," she said. "Do you really love me?"

His face softened. "I really do." Pulling a chair over to the fan, he retrieved her lace panties and handed them to her.

Ellie began to dress, biting her lower lip. "Do you really, *really* love me?"

Mark's smile widened even as he surveyed his shredded shirt in the mirror. "You know I do. Remind me to buy you a pair of gloves right away."

The commotion was getting louder, the sound of many voices raised. Mark pulled on his jacket, straightened his tie and walked toward the door. "Something's going on."

"Mark!" Ellie grabbed his hand and fought to keep the desperation out of her voice. "Please tell me there's nothing I could do to make you stop loving me."

He turned toward her again, taking her face in his hands. "Sweetheart, there's nothing you could do to make me stop loving you." He lowered his mouth to hers for a quick, loving kiss.

A knock sounded at the door. "Mark?" Monica asked from the other side, her voice urgent.

"Promise?" Ellie asked, gripping his hands.

"Yes, I promise, Ellie." He turned to open the door, then noticed the wrapped portrait Ellie had brought. "What's that?"

Ellie just shrugged her shoulders, smiling wide.

"The last time I saw that look, Esmerelda had gone fishing."

"Mark?" Monica's voice was insistent, her knocking louder.

He opened the door. "What's all the noise, Monica?"

His secretary wore an unreadable expression, her eyes wide. "You're needed in the boardroom. *Right away.*"

"Is something wrong?" he asked, concern written on his face.

Monica glanced at Ellie, and Ellie saw raw admiration on the woman's face. "Not everyone would think so."

Mark walked out the door and strode down the hall toward the boardroom. Ellie hesitated, but Monica grabbed her arm and pulled her along. Ellie's mind raced. How was she going to explain this one?

She stepped into the crowded room a split second behind Mark, in time to see his eyes land on the nearly life-size sprawling nude. A roomful of suited men and women roared, Ray and Patrick both bent double, tears streaming down their faces.

Mark's jaw fell, and his mouth worked up and down, but no sound came out. He turned his head slowly to look at Ellie, and she winced, taking a half step back. This was going to be an interesting relationship.

His eyes were round in disbelief, his hands clenched in fists at his sides. "Ellie," he said, his voice ominously low. "What the hell is that?"

All eyes turned to Ellie and the room quieted, poised for her answer. Swallowing, Ellie tried to gather her courage. She lifted her chin and smiled nervously at her glowering husband-to-be.

"That, as everyone can see," she said brightly, sweeping her arm in a grand gesture, "is one well-hung portrait."